ONE

Because Lydia didn't have arms or legs, she shelled out three thousand bucks to a washed-up middleweight named Cap to give her ex-husband the beating of his life. Before the car wreck took her limbs, she was in control of Ronnie. She kept the house, the Lexus, and got a generous check every month. Thankfully they never had kids, so the money was hers to do with as she pleased—Caribbean trips, an interior designer, acceptance in the power circle of Gulf Coast doctors, lawyers, casino investors. Then an SUV turned her sporty coupe to scrap and Lydia to a quad amputee.

She sat in her wheelchair near the open windows of her home a couple of blocks from the beach in Biloxi, the curtains slow-dancing in the spring breeze and brushing her face. Her rubber arms and legs were sculpted to resemble Jayne Mansfield's, at least giving an illusion of fullness. The doctors said other prosthetics could give her back some mobility—hooks or robot fingers, a slow clunky walk. In the end she chose grace over function.

Ronnie splurged in helping her wire the house so she could work the doors, the lights, and the phone with voice commands. The chair was state of the art with sip-and-puff control through a straw. Underneath her ex's helpful façade was the same condescending bastard. He skipped alimony payments, dropped in unannounced at all hours, scheduled her appointments for therapy and doctors. Slipped back into controlling her life, exactly what she wanted to escape by divorcing him. She needed him again and hated every moment.

When they'd met in the late-eighties, he was a flashy guy hiding his cocaine trade under legit investments, easy to do with casino resorts beginning to flourish along the coast. Lydia loved his easy-going "take what I want" attitude—Ronnie wanted her and she melted for him. After they were married, other women kept melting for him and he kept taking them. Maybe if he had hidden the evidence a little more, she wouldn't have been so angry. Instead, Ronnie flaunted the affairs, dared Lydia to make a fuss and give up her new waking-dream lifestyle. So she fucked his best friend, a lawyer, who helped her bust the pre-nup wide open and get a third of everything Ronnie had his fingers in.

Ronnie actually seemed impressed. He never showed anger towards her, but every conversation after the divorce felt strange, like he believed they were playing a game where one would win, one would lose. Some nights after the nurse put her to bed, she even wondered how "accidental" the crash was. Still, nothing compared to the night a couple of weeks ago when Ronnie appeared at her door drunk with a coed barfly. He disconnected Lydia's chair and made her watch the make-out session that followed.

God, she hated him for that. God, she wanted him so badly, wanted to feel his hands and lips all over her again, his dick deep inside her.

After fucking the D-cup bitch, Ronnie zipped up, reconnected the chair, and the couple left without a word.

He deserved every bruise this boxer could dish out. She closed her eyes, dialed the number she'd called once before, and told Cap to come pick up his money.

"Punish the prick," she said.

When Ronnie found out what Lydia was planning, he paid the same fighter an extra grand to take a dive. Cap was fine with that—it was how he got washed up in the first place. The sure money was in the losing. If he wanted pride, he'd catch a big fish and hang it on his wall. Pride didn't pay the bills.

What Lydia didn't know was that the guy who gave her Cap's number was a close friend, and Cap had taken dives for Ronnie before in fights at the casino in Bay St. Louis. Hell, even the divorce settlement was okayed by Ronnie before his friend made it look like fine lawyering on her behalf.

Ronnie told him, "If she tries to fuck you, go ahead. Make sure you tape it."

The cocaine dealing had gone south in the mid-nineties, but Ronnie poured enough into the stock market and sold at the right time so he'd never have to work again. Not that he ever worked much anyway. He grew bored of gambling, snorting, and fucking nearly every day, no thrill to it anymore. Dealing with the aftermath of Lydia's wreck gave him something fun to do. He saw it in her eyes. It was torture.

Cap called Ronnie to set up the fake beating. "You want it outside, inside?"

"Outside. I want somebody to tape it, let Lydia watch her cash fail her."

Ronnie then called Alan Crabtree, a guy on the fringes of the underworld who made a career of taking little jobs like this—just give him a video camera, a time and place, and a couple of twenties. Ronnie met with Alan for lunch at a Mexican joint on the beach in Biloxi. Alan arrived early, a few Coronas in him already and pulling the self-pity routine on a middle-aged blond barfly chain-smoking Turkish cigarettes by the time Ronnie showed.

Alan was five-seven and he weighed two-seventy. When drunk, he told people, "I wanted to be a jockey. I know all about horses, love them, oh I do. The weight, though. That's a gland thing."

Ronnie tapped Alan's shoulder, stopping him mid-sentence. Alan told the barfly, "Wait here, okay?"

She said, "I'm not going anywhere, with or without you." Then she asked the bartender for a Rum and Coke.

Ronnie and Alan took a corner booth. The waitress brought more Coronas, chips, salsa. Ronnie ordered fajitas. Alan wanted a chimichanga. He wore his usual XXL Polo pullover, sweat rings threatening to spread across his chest.

"We're going to do this at my place in the parking lot. We want it quick, sometime when there's not a lot of people around, after they leave for work," Ronnie said.

"That's a nice shirt. Is that designer?" Alan shook some jalapeno juice into the salsa.

"Probably." Ronnie was beach bum chic—shirt hanging out, khaki shorts, dark hair slicked back, cell phone clipped on a belt loop. "You listening to me? The camera's in my car. One of the small ones you hold like this."

Ronnie picked up a coaster, held the left and right sides.

"With the little screen on it?"

"Yeah. Be there at nine tomorrow morning. Here's my apartment building's address." He slid a napkin with ink bleeds across to Alan. "Don't film until a couple punches have been thrown. We want it to look like you just happened by."

"My money?"

Ronnie pulled a folded twenty from his shirt pocket. "The other half after she gets the tape. Plus I'm buying this lunch."

Alan smiled, held the Corona up in a toast, and said, "*Mucho gracias.*"

Alan Crabtree hated kissing the asses of the well-to-do. He didn't have much choice, especially after blowing a blackjack dealer gig at a reservation casino in north Mississippi. He had hoped the job might lead to a chance to come to Biloxi, where the pay was better and there were nicer places to waste it on food and beer. After getting eighty-sixed for *maybe* being a little too helpful with players to get better tips, he decided to try his luck further south anyway.

He was fucked from the start. All the casinos along the coast knew his story already and turned him down flat. Even at one on the Back Bay, small and already worn out after one decade of business, he got to the second interview before they somehow found out. As the weeks went by, his already a hefty gut kept spreading, and the easiest work so far was these Dixie Mafia odd jobs. Fucking rednecks playing gangsters. To their faces, Alan was all respect. Behind their backs, he felt dirtier than the whores who sucked their cocks. Another couple of months of this was all he could take. He needed a real job, something legal, something he could be proud of.

When Alan got home after meeting with Ronnie, a Jeep was waiting on the curb with two guys leaning against it. He pulled his almost brand-new Monte Carlo into the driveway, stopped short of the garage, and got out. The two guys, Terry and Lancaster, stumbled up to meet him. They looked like frat boys, only a little older, with Ray Bans and form fitting caps, bills curved just right. They smelled like too much sweet cologne, wore two-day stubble on their faces.

Terry and Lancaster had given Alan a great deal on the Monte Carlo and wanted the last payment, which was a month late. They sold cars that they stole from the side of Interstate 10, spending most days riding the stretch between Biloxi and Mobile looking for breakdowns on the shoulders. Sometimes people abandoned nice ones, like Toyotas or Ford trucks or even an Infiniti, while going for help. Now that more people carried cell phones, finding nicer rides became tougher, the drivers calling and waiting at the car. Most breakdowns were blown tires, dead batteries, or no gas. Terry and Lancaster carried spare tires, new batteries, and some gas cans, fixed the easy ones and sold them to people who didn't mind paying cash for hot cars.

Alan got them to split his bill to three due dates. The price for not keeping up was serious tire iron lacerations, jumper cables clipped to your ass, a shot to the nuts with an aluminum bat, or repossession.

"Guys, tomorrow. Promise." He held out his free hand, pleading.

"Look at this, you've got enough for a new video camera. What, you got a date tonight? Need to document the moment?"

"This ain't mine."

"The car's not yet, either." Lancaster leaned in close, sniffed. "Smells like you've had a few too many beers. What are you doing driving *our* car lit up?"

Alan shook his head, hugged the camera to his chest. "It's a job I've got for tomorrow. Go tape a special event for a few minutes, and they'll give me forty bucks. I can give *you* forty bucks."

"You owe us six hundred," Terry said.

"I was going to talk him up afterwards. See, he needs the tape so bad, he'll pay whatever I ask."

Lancaster and Terry passed a smile between them. Terry said, "That's quite a jump there."

"Doesn't sound economically sound."

"Think he'll succeed?"

"Not a vampire's chance at daybreak."

No neighbors out, no gun handy—Alan's only one was a .22 rifle in the closet. He hadn't bought ammo in three years. Sweat rolled down his face. He was about to get the crap beat out of him.

Lancaster said, "Tell you what. I feel, um, I guess it's compassion. I say he's playing straight with us. Let's give him a day."

Terry crossed his arms, rolled his tongue around the inside of his lips. He said, "I don't know. He still needs a warning."

"Agreed."

Lancaster grabbed Alan's wrist and batted the camcorder into the grass. Alan whined, watched it fall. With both of the fat man's arms pinned, Lancaster pushed him to the driveway, face down. He grabbed Alan's hair and grated his cheek back and forth against the concrete. The pain burned white hot, ratcheting up with each yank across the pavement. Alan closed his eyes and screamed.

They eased off after a minute, started towards the Jeep. Terry shouted, "Tomorrow night, all six hundred. No excuses. Or we'll take the car."

Alan opened his eyes, pushed himself up. There was a red smear on the concrete. He was dripping. He smacked a palm onto his cheek, which made the burning worse, then watched the Jeep roll away before running inside to the bathroom and washing his face. He poured some peroxide on it—mistake!—patting it cool until the bleeding stopped, smudged some ointment on. He stared into the mirror, tears in his eyes, wondering how much worse he would feel tomorrow night when the money was due but not there. Then he remembered the camera.

He found it in the grass. The viewscreen was cracked and the black plastic case was scuffed. Alan thought Ronnie would deduct the damage from his pay. He might even owe Ronnie for repairs.

Alan sat in his car across from the Sea Crest Apartments the next morn-ing eating a second egg and sausage biscuit while waiting for the scuffle. The night before, he tested the camera in his backyard, taped some birds, and it worked fine. He wore amber shades, baggy khakis, a T-shirt, and a blue plastic visor. There was also a piece of gauze taped to his cheek. The windows were rolled down, sea breeze smelling fishy fresh.

Cap pulled into the lot and got out of his car, looking like a *Dragnet* leftover in slacks and a tight Polo shirt, hair greased, leaning on the trunk. He glanced at his watch. Alan hoped it would be a convincing fight. Nothing worse than taking a con to the sucker and the sucker see-ing right through it like plastic wrap. Who would she blame then? The man with the tape, that's who.

Alan watched Ronnie slink to his Mercedes—oh so cool—then saw Cap, gave a thumbs up. Cap started towards him, and when he was in front of the guy, stood for a minute talking, Alan not hearing the words. Ronnie pounded his chest lightly, and Cap shoved him. Ronnie wailed away, landed some good slaps, a big shove. Hard to believe little Ronnie could get the Cap off balance like that. Cap balled his fists and landed a punch in Ronnie's gut. That's when Alan lifted the camera and turned it on. Cap worked the kidneys. Ronnie kicked Cap's shins. Cap was look-ing for a head shot, like he forgot this was a game and took it seriously. The low battery light blinked on. Alan groaned and shook his head. He forgot to recharge it last night, plus the jolt might have damaged it. He didn't know how much longer the thing would film. Cap finally got a tag on Ronnie's face. Ronnie yelped. Nobody was around, but Alan thought he saw a few curtain peepers in the apartments. Ronnie rammed Cap, shoved him back towards the stairs, secluded where Alan couldn't see.

Alan jumped out of his car and followed, straight arming the camera like cops did guns on TV. He thought something didn't look right—Ronnie making Cap angry instead of telling him it was time to drop, like Ronnie wanted his ass kicked after all.

He caught sight of them when he reached the Mercedes, Cap and Ronnie standing a few feet apart by the stairs. Ronnie reached under his shirt, pulled a pistol from his waistband. Alan prepped to run, gunfire the ultimate attention grabber, but he waited, trusting that Ronnie had planned it all to the tee. There wasn't a more immediate way for to extort six hundred bucks, so Alan stuck with it, zoomed in.

Cap swooped in lightning-fast and slapped the gun away, then did a brutal karate chop to Ronnie's throat. Looked like army training, that heavy special forces shit. Ronnie grabbed his throat, wheezed. He doubled over and fell to the ground. Alan ran to them, covered his hand with his shirttail, and picked up the pistol.

"I think it's a fake. A pellet gun."

"What?"

"No clip." Alan shook Ronnie's shoulder. "He'll be okay?"

"No, he's dead."

Alan leaned close, didn't touch, listened for breathing. It wasn't there. "How do you know he's dead?"

Cap sighed, shook his fingers. "I've only tried that move on two other people, and both died. That's what you do when someone points a gun at you. The training took over. Sorry."

"We've got to get him out of here. Like, *way* out of here." Alan felt Ronnie's pockets for keys, pulled them out. "Let's get him to the car, you drive down the street, let me move mine."

They draped Ronnie's arms over their shoulders and carried him between them, then sat him in the Mercedes' passenger seat, strapped him in. His head lolled back and his mouth was wide open. Cap drove Ronnie's car, followed Alan to the mall. Alan parked and got in Ronnie's backseat.

"So, how do we get rid of him?" Cap asked.

"Take him out of state? Dump him in a river? Chop him up?"

"I'm not doing *that*. It ain't like I stabbed him or something. Look at him, clean that way. He'll have a bruise, that's about all."

Alan sat back, thought about the situation a few minutes. His six hundred was gone for sure. He looked out the window at his Monte Carlo—a great machine. He kept up the maintenance, washed it, kept the inside clean. It was the best car Alan ever owned, for an unreal price, about to slip away from him, and his good health along with it. Then he got an idea.

"Cap, I'm taking my car. You follow me. I think this'll work."

Later that afternoon, Alan rang Lydia's doorbell. After a moment, the lock clicked and the door swung open, nobody behind it. Only a dimly lit hall until a wheelchair rolled out of a side room carrying a petite woman, blond hair bundled on top, plastic framed glasses. Wearing a headset mike, she puffed on a big plastic straw that trailed into the back of her chair, where it connected to a small box above the motor.

What made Alan really lift his eyebrows was what he didn't expect to see. Under a long silk skirt were two legs, crossed, barefoot. There were arms in the sleeves of her sweater, elbows on the armrests, hands together in her lap. She noticed him looking and smiled.

"Prosthetics. Makes me feel like a real person. People who don't know can't tell with a glance." Lydia sipped the straw, causing the chair to roll backwards. "Please, come in. What happened to your face?"

His fingers brushed the gauze. "I fell, skinned my cheek. Nothing serious."

She led him to a bright living room, all the windows open, curtains like ghosts in the breeze. There was a leather recliner at the end of the couch, and Lydia rolled next to it. Alan sat close at the edge of the couch, sank into the deep cushion. He set the camera on the coffee table in front of him.

"I was surprised you called, Mr. Sony. Not your real name, is it?"

Alan shook his head. He got it off the camera, spur of the moment thing.

"Would you like a drink? Have to get it yourself, though."

Alan felt embarrassed, couldn't look at her for too long. She was beautiful, but obviously tired in spirit. The legs were perfect—made to order. He tried to visualize the nubs.

"I have a tape. Your husband, I found out later. I happened to be driving by this morning—"

"No lies. Not a good way to start. He hired you?"

She surprised him into the truth before he thought better about it. "Well, um, sure. That's it."

"Did he get to Cap? Rig the fight?" The look on her face was severe, about to break down and cry. "I hired the wrong man, didn't I? You're here to show how my money was wasted."

Alan shrugged. "Listen a minute, okay? Things didn't go as planned. Ronnie tried pulling a gun on Cap, and Cap toasted him. Crushed his windpipe. We knew it was rigged, but pulling a gun, geez. Cap didn't sign up to *die*, right?"

Lydia nodded. News of her husband's death seemed to soften the lines on her face. It was peace. Alan wondered how much of a bastard Ronnie had been to her.

"I know some guys, always boosting cars from the side of the interstate. All the breakdowns people leave for a while. So, I'm thinking about this, and it hits me that we should strap Ronnie in, leave him on the side of the road. Who would notice? Except those car thieves, maybe."

"No way to trace it back?"

"If they find him quickly, sure, all the lab work. I cleaned out everything best I could. Motive, stuff like that, I'm clean. I hope you paid Cap in cash."

"Of course. They won't connect it to me. Or you. And Cap?"

"Well, it's his head, right? He would have sung if caught, and then they come looking for you. So Cap is sharing the car with Ronnie. I told him Ronnie's gun was a fake—it wasn't. After setting up Ronnie, with Cap still leaning through the driver's window, I put the gun in Ronnie's hand and shot the poor son of a bitch in the chest."

Alan said it like a tough guy but he remembered how he flinched when the shot went off, how he couldn't open his eyes for a minute or two after, how he gagged and nearly threw up on the way back to his car. He'd never killed a man before and couldn't lose the image of Cap's shocked dead face.

Lydia said, "There are so many mistakes in that. They'll see through it."

Alan shrugged, cleared his throat. "Best I could do off the top of my head."

"May I see the tape?"

They watched it, from the birds in Alan's backyard at the beginning right until the point where Ronnie pulled the gun and the battery died. Alan took the tape from the VCR, said he was going to burn it later. Then he waited, hoping she would offer.

She did. "I have to thank you. I feel much better. You would accept a token of my appreciation?"

"Sure, of course."

"Any particular needs?"

"Six hundred dollars."

Lydia blinked, surprised. "So exact. Gambling debt?"

"Something like that."

Lydia leaned her head towards the bar. She spoke into her headset mike, and Alan heard another click.

"There's a safe behind the bottles on the second shelf. Take what you need, close it when you're done."

In the small safe, there were four piles of cash, all about half a foot tall. Alan counted out his six hundred, closed the door, then showed Lydia, letting her know he was honest. She nodded, led him to the front door. Before stepping out, Alan said, "Mind a question?"

"Go right ahead."

"Why did you hate Ronnie so much? I mean, he cause you to lose your limbs?"

Lydia grinned. "No, not that. We were already divorced when this happened. Car wreck. Before that, he mailed alimony checks—big ones. After the accident, he tried to smooth things over, wanted to take care of me. For a while I couldn't resist. Still, the way he did things…"

"Yeah, I understand."

"No, not yet. See, one night he brought a *date* over, both of them drunk. They started making out on the couch. Started peeling clothes off, started drilling her. It took an hour, like some porno flick, all those different positions."

"What a bastard."

"Oh yeah. It turned me on," Lydia watched Alan's face. "When they were done, they left without a word, left me alone. That was what hurt the most. Mr. Sony, do you know how *long* it's been for me? Don't you find me the least bit attractive?"

Alan didn't move or speak for a long moment, then he smiled and closed the front door, leaned over and kissed Lydia's cheek.

He said, "Lead the way."

After midnight, Alan drove home in his Monte Carlo with the windows down, rock radio station blasting Sammy Hagar, thinking that once he paid those guys off for the car, he was going to put in a CD player. And he would definitely see Lydia again very soon.

TWO

Terry and Lancaster were installing a battery into a Chevy Cavalier they'd found near the Franklin Creek exit on the shoulder of I-10 when the State Trooper's patrol car rolled up and parked between the Chevy and Lancaster's F-150 pick-up. He punched the siren, then sat in the car a couple of minutes while big rigs, cars, and SUVs whizzed past like roaring smudges.

Terry leaned against the Chevy, hands in the pockets of his Abercrombie and Finch khaki shorts, an oversized bowling shirt covering a beer gut, and a cap pulled low above his eyes. He stared at the trooper, blonde mustache and small eyes, hard to read. Lancaster stepped from behind the raised hood, a tight Nautica T-shirt stretched over muscled-up chest and shoulders, in cut-off jeans. Short dark hair and a face that narrowed to a strong pointy chin. He wiped his hands on a rag, shrugged, then ducked back to the battery.

The trooper, a tall thin man, stepped from his car and stalked over to the guys, leaving plenty of room in case he had to draw down on them. The shoulder of the road was wide with a narrow grassy ditch separating it from the woods.

He nodded. "Morning."

Terry nodded back. "We're doing fine. Don't need any help."

"What's the problem, anyway?"

"Damn battery, or the alternator. I can't tell. My friend brought a new battery so we can at least get it back to the house."

The trooper shook his head, the hat teetering. He laughed a bit, moved his right hand to his pistol.

"Bullshit," he said, doing Gleason from *Smokey and the Bandit*. "You boys are trying to sell me a *fab-ree-cation*."

Terry pushed himself off the car, nice and slow. "What are you talking about?"

"This one?" The trooper pointed at the car. "It's my *wife's* car, you dumb fuck. She called me an hour ago, and I dropped her off at home, came back to take a look."

Terry squinted. "You sure about that?"

The trooper reached for his handcuffs. "Both of you, against the car."

Terry pulled his hands from his pockets, turned and placed them on top of the driver's side door. "What did we really do? Just trying to help, save you the trouble of doing the work yourself."

"You lied to me."

"A little, but no harm done. You get a free battery."

The trooper stepped closer, an inch away from cuffing. Lancaster's arm arched from behind the hood, hand wrapped around a small .380. Two shots like balloons popping. The bullets smashed into the trooper's shoulder and chest, dropping him. He was still strong enough to yank his gun free, get off a shot that missed Terry by a hair, clanged off the hood and shattered the windshield.

Terry shrunk. "Jesus! What the fuck?"

Lancaster moved fast as the trooper's free hand groped for his radio. He stepped on the trooper's wounded shoulder, grabbed the gun and twisted as the grip gave way to pain. He slipped the gun into his waistband, took the radio, then dragged the trooper by the shirt off the road, through the grassy ditch and into the woods.

Terry watched the road for brake lights, see if anyone had noticed and would stop, turn around. A few minutes went by. Nothing. Six years working together, Lancaster always high strung but never homicidal. Terry thought he was too rough with Crabtree the day before, but killing a cop? It freaked him out. He followed Lancaster into the woods. They were sweating in the July heat, over a hundred, and the shade of the trees calmed their nerves a little.

Terry said, "Shit, in front of God and everybody. What the hell?"

"We were so damn close. His wife's car? Come on, you couldn't talk our way out of that one."

"You didn't let me try."

"He was about to cuff you. Hey, no need to thank me."

"Call it a loss now. Blows out the windshield, shit. We've got to book it out of here."

"What about the battery?" Lancaster said. He stomped the trooper's shoulder again. High-pitched scream. The blood was soaking his shirt, spreading fast.

"Was that necessary?"

Lancaster shrugged.

"Get the battery double-fast. I'll take him in his cruiser, you follow in the truck."

"What's the plan?"

Terry shook his head. "I can think better driving."

Six years conning, three years boosting cars from the Mississippi road-sides and they'd never been caught. When trouble closed in, Terry was good at charming their way out, a natural born con artist. Even though Lancaster always carried a piece, shooting the trooper was the first time he fired it while working with his friend.

Maybe Terry could have smoothed it out. Lancaster admitted that as he tailed the cruiser off the Interstate exit ramp and north on Franklin Creek Road, a badly paved two lane that twisted up into the country. Lots of nice homes and big yards, then there were old trailers, small churches, tiny gas stations, torn papers and beer cans circling tree trunks.

Maybe. But Lancaster was bored. Working with Terry made them de-cent money if middle-class was the goal. They needed to risk a lot more to get the big payoff. Hit a casino, a bank, or put the big squeeze on a millionaire. Lancaster even suggested they get back into the drug scene, deal in heroin and meth. Terry had laughed at the idea. Laughed, he sure fucking did. He won't be doing that anymore. Lancaster grinned, thinking it was a test. He hoped the boy could handle a new way of doing things. Lancaster liked to work the same way he liked having sex—rough.

His oil-stained hands tightened around the steering wheel as he re-membered two years in Angola prison, his foot pressed the gas a little heavier. The truck gurgled and responded, closing the gap between the vehicles. Best thing to do would be drop the car in a lake, burn the body, scatter the bones as far apart as possible. And if Terry disagreed, maybe Lancaster would have to kill him, too.

Terry knew there was a pond around the area big enough to sink the car, and he was headed that way. Figured out how to turn off the radio after already knocking out the camera that had caught every moment of the encounter. The car smelled like aftershave.

He glanced in the rearview. Lancaster rode his bumper, a severe look on his face. Terry was always afraid his partner would crack and go on a psycho rampage he had only witnessed once, near sunrise in the bathroom of a motel. Lancaster dunked a barfly's head into the tub filled with ice cold water, demanding she tell him his breath wasn't so bad and show it by kissing him. She did. She was shaking. He paid her and she backed out of the room holding her clothes to her stomach.

Lancaster had told him it was a bad night, too much gin. Terry thought the beast was always there under the surface, alcohol just an easy excuse. What they were doing with the cars, like with Crabtree, was supposed to be about intimidation, psychology. Lately, Lancaster was quick to go nuclear, and if he kept it up, they were sure to get caught. Terry was beginning to believe he should break up the team, go back to college for those final classes he needed for his criminal justice degree, and join the other side. He thought he'd be great at it because by being a criminal, he knew how they thought.

The trooper stirred in the backseat, startling Terry. Lucky he cuffed the guy, a precaution, even though he thought the trooper was nearly done bleeding all his blood. Terry glanced at him, then back at the road, which had ended at a T, a Baptist church straight ahead. Terry turned right, then looked at the trooper again. This time, the eyes were open and staring back.

"It's not fair. I'm going to die over this, and it's not fair because you two punks got lucky. Not even a real shoot out."

"I'm sorry, really," Terry said, surprised how much he really meant it. "But don't say we got lucky because you got sloppy."

A pained chuckle, sharp breath. "Say it's some of both, then. A shoot out with dangerous criminals, okay, I can live with dying like that."

Terry tapped the steering wheel, nervous rhythm, and kept quiet, hoping the trooper would shut up and keep bleeding. He wished Lancaster would back off his tail.

"My wife, my son—"

Terry said, "All right, I got that whole hero thing you want. You probably tell them every night how you love them, 'In case I don't come back.' Like you get anything more than drunks and pot runners."

"I don't have to listen to this."

"Hey, you're right. That was too harsh, man." Terry wondered if he should let the guy write a final letter or something.

The pond wasn't far. Terry remembered this road now, one he'd driven down many nights while seeing a girl up this way back when he was in high school, just got a car. She had long dark hair, country girl accent, liked to go barefoot. Terry loved that perfect walking cliché. They used to make out in her bedroom while her parents were home, the radio loud on a contemporary gospel station. Yeah, she used to live off this road.

"Can't you at least make it *look* like I died in a real fight, like I had a chance?"

"Oh, man," Terry sighed, again thinking, *Might as well give him a last request.*

"Let me call in for help, and they'll find me dead. Please don't let them figure out the truth."

Terry blinked, blinked, held his eyes shut, then opened them. Another look in the mirror. Lancaster still right on his back bumper, panic turned to anger turned to determination. The trooper was right. It wasn't fair. Terry thought about it for another minute, then asked the trooper, "You got another gun in here?"

Lancaster had an urge to the bump the damn cruiser, forgetting it was Terry in there instead of a couple buzzcut troopers with those dead eyes that always looked at him like he was a bug on somebody's burger, crawling around in the mustard.

Then there was a commotion, looked like Terry was slapping at the wire mesh behind him, and the brake lights flashed quick and the car swerved and veered onto the roadside, the steep incline, stopping half a foot from a tree. Lancaster pulled over and put the truck in park, jumped out as Terry sprang from the car, the trooper's gun held high, a small video camera in his other hand, trying to cover his head and run low to the ground.

"Another gun!" Terry yelled. "He hid a fucking gun!"

Lancaster looked at the trooper, propped against the door and pointing a .38 revolver at the window. One, two, three shots slammed into the window, wild spider-webbing all over it, until one slug made it out and dropped into the ground, puff of dirt rising. Lancaster felt the adrenaline rush build and do his thinking for him. He took four steps closer to the door, unloading his gun into the trooper's body. It jumped like popcorn the first two shots, then took the rest lying still.

Terry ran up behind Lancaster. "We've got to go. I'll wipe off my prints and we're out of here. He's called for back-up."

"Where'd he get the radio?"

Terry twisted his mouth. "They carry two of everything."

"No they don't."

Terry grabbed Lancaster's shirt and pulled, saying, "A radio under the backseat. Get in the truck. Let's get the hell out of here."

Terry turned for the truck, took two steps, then heard more shots, flinched and spun. Lancaster had fired at the car, making big holes in the doors.

"What was that?" Terry said.

"I thought he moved."

"Whatever. I swear, though, he had me dead to rights for a second there, point blank. Ready to roll?"

Lancaster thought something about the story wasn't fitting. Just a feeling, but it would keep him out of jail at least tonight, and maybe they could lay low for a while. A lot less work to do since they wouldn't have to drown the car and burn the trooper. So things worked out well enough. He walked back to his truck, slipped inside.

Terry wiped the door handle, the steering wheel, the trooper's gun. He tossed it into the dead man's lap, which Lancaster thought was a bit weird. Then he noticed the dead man's hands, free and spread wide.

Terry climbed into the truck, held the camera in his lap, and Lancaster looked at him before pulling the stick into gear. "I thought you cuffed him?"

"I did."

A grin curled. "You're going to start lying to me now. What really happened? Or how about I just watch the tape?"

Terry's fingers tightened on the camera. He met his friend's eyes and held the gaze, dead serious. "You remember that girl you almost drowned?"

It took him a moment. "Yeah."

"Remember when her sister found you at the bar that night, followed us outside and plugged you with the Tazer? Then kicked the shit of you? You said that if anyone asked, I should say you got jumped by bikers in the restroom. Let's say it was something like that."

Lancaster nodded, accelerated and made a sharp turn, headed south. "Good enough."

Terry said, "You'll need to bleach your hair. We're going to ground for a while."

"Why do I have to bleach? Why can't you dye yours?"

"I don't know. My way makes more sense."

THREE

Alan Crabtree played video poker in the bar of the Pirate's Bay casino at two in the afternoon, always a bit tense in these places because he never knew when the eye in the sky would recognize him and get him tossed. It happened twice already, both at the big places with loose slots, big comfortable chairs. Since the Coast wasn't big on horse racing, video poker was a decent substitute.

Pretty soon, he wouldn't need to. He was spending so many nights with Lydia, they decided to cancel the nursing service that usually helped her with morning routines, daily chores, and helping her to bed, and let Alan move in to handle all that until he found a steady job worthy of his talents. He couldn't wait, really, except when he was sitting at a poker machine. Weigh poker versus Lydia, though, it wasn't much of a contest.

In the meantime, Alan had spent most days here and a few other Coast casinos that still hadn't tossed him. He'd paid Terry and Lancaster the six hundred he owed for the car, didn't have other bills besides the rent on his house, and Lydia helped out with cash. One thought he had was maybe seeing if one of the gaming schools needed a teacher for black-jack. They couldn't keep him from that, right? It wasn't the same as real dealing. Lydia seemed to think it was a good idea. Actually, she didn't say much about it at all, Alan now second-guessing her every word.

An upscale redneck—clean jeans, an ironed Western shirt, a Dale Jr. cap covering what looked like not much hair—took the stool beside him. Alan *felt* this guy beside him, literally, being pretty wide already, although he was down to two-fifty on that low-carb diet, toning up since he'd been seeing Lydia. No one else around except an oldster at the far end of the bar telling the bartender about some tarot card reading he got over the phone. The bartender nodded and said, "Is that right?" occasionally, not listening.

The oldster said, "I asked her about you, too. You're gonna die."

"Is that right?"

All those empty seats, and this cowboy wanted to crowd Alan, maybe turn on the intimidation. It wasn't necessary. Alan scared easily, even more so since shooting Cap.

"You the guy who got rid of Ronnie?" The cowboy said. His eyes were magnified behind thick glasses. Looked the same age as Lydia, early thirties, except for the receding hairline.

"Sorry? I don't understand." Alan picked up his Corona, took a sip and fought hard not to shake. The lime did a little dance in the bottle. He hoped the cowboy wouldn't notice. That and the sweat rings under the arms of his big yellow Polo shirt.

"You lie badly, Alan." The guy's voice was hokey. "You and Cap took the bastard out a couple months ago, and then you made it look like Cap was the only player, shot him cold and left him next to Ronnie in a car."

Alan reflex-nodded before he could think. "Sounds crazy."

He wondered what this guy knew. Only Lydia and he were in on the real details. Unless she—why would she? She swore it was their secret, wiped clean from their minds as far as the world was concerned. He believed her until this guy showed up.

Alan took another sip, longer this time, then played five more quarters. He caught a break, instant three of a kind off sixes. Then he doubled up, sighed while doing it, and the computer drew a fucking queen of hearts. Alan's card was an eight of clubs. Jesus, this wasn't anything like betting the horses. There was a greyhound track over in Mobile, nowhere near the same thrill.

The cowboy said, "I'm not going to walk away and pretend it didn't happen. You want my business, you'd better stop the secret agent bullshit and talk to me."

Alan turned his face to the guy. "What do you mean by business?"

The cowboy grinned. "You want to take a booth over there, a little more private?"

Alan looked back. The dark booths were empty, all curved benches around round tables that faced the stage over the bar, near a small space cleared for dancing. A big screen TV off to the side ran a March Madness game, LSU and Ohio State. Alan's cup held just under sixty bucks in quarters, breaking fairly even after an hour of play, and he had all afternoon to keep at it before going to Lydia's.

He thought, *So why not listen for a few minutes?*

The cowboy slipped off the stool and made his way to a table while Alan signaled for the bartender, got another Corona, then turned and asked the other guy if he wanted something.

"A Bud Light."

The bartender shook his head. "You have to pay for it if you're not gambling."

"He lost big downstairs," Alan said.

The bartender stared and waited until Alan dug a handful of quarters from his bucket and counted out four dollars. The bartender swept them away, then handed over both bottles. Alan was a regular here, saw this bartender every few days, and was surprised to get this treatment. Something about the cowboy, must've been.

At the booth, Alan set the Bud Light on the table, then scooched into the seat, staring the cowboy down. The air smelled like hope, a special scent they piped in, so Alan heard. The noise was a constant one-note doorbell that gamblers were used to, letting it subconsciously blend into their minds so that they dream about the noise and are drawn back later.

The cowboy took off his cap—bald up top and thinning all over, like Alan guessed—wiped his forehead, then snugged it back on. "Right to it. Call me Cowboy, no need for my real name in this."

"I'll call you Redneck."

"Cow. Boy," he said, slow and hard.

Alan shook his head. " 'Cowboy' will cost you extra. 'Redneck' gets you a discount."

"Think you're funny?"

"No. You know *my* real name. How about that? Price goes up again."

It was fun goofing with the guy and watching him get his feelings injured. The cowboy tried hard to keep things bottled. Played nice. Alan figured he was about to ask for something important and dead serious.

"I've got a partner in my operation. What that operation is, you don't need to know."

Drugs, Alan thought immediately. *Meth, heroin, crack, X. Which one?*

The cowboy said, "Now the partner's got some new friends. Some guys out of Pensacola want him to help move some heavier weight. That's fine, if he wants to cut and run, sure, but he needs *seed* money to get into the game. And where do you think he's finding it?"

"His ass?" Alan wished the cowboy wouldn't ask questions. What was the point?

The guy wagged a finger. "Funny shit, yeah, you *are* funny. He's taking the money from our operation. Skimming it, thinking I won't notice. I followed up, talked to some clients, some of our assistants. He's raised the price without telling me, keeps the surplus."

He leaned back and crossed his arms, raised his eyebrows like he expected Alan to say *That rat bastard thief!* when Alan really thought *Good for him.*

"And?" Alan said.

"You don't have be rude."

Alan lifted his bottle, took a long, long sip, held up a *Wait a minute* palm. Then he slammed the bottle to the table, sounded a loud rolling belch, cleared his throat and said, "And?"

Redneck tossed his head back and murmured *Fuck this shit* before saying, "I want you to get rid of him. How much for that?"

Alan went cold, suddenly realizing what this was about. Until then, he was thinking just another odd job. Did Lydia pimp him out as an assassin? Jesus, he couldn't do that. He felt more afraid than usual, played steady. Instead of the hoods doling out little scraps, fall guy things if he were to have gotten caught, offing Cap put him a few steps up the ladder now. It was all built on lies—he killed Cap, sure, but Cap killed Ronnie and if the plan had gone right, no one should have died anyway.

"How much?" Redneck said again, his expression hyped, tight, waiting for the phone to ring, tell him his daddy was dead. One of those.

Alan said, "You're not really losing anything are you? Your cut stays the same."

"We shook hands on fifty-fifty, and I'm a man of my word."

"If he dies, you get it all." Alan felt he was about to get another pitiful justification, so he jumped in with the same price Lydia paid Cap to beat up her ex-husband Ronnie, but not kill him. "Three thousand."

Redneck nodded slowly. It was like he wandered into an expensive store, picked up something small and saw it was worth a month's pay. Don't mention it, look shocked, talk about how fucking much else you could buy instead. Pass for rich by looking bored.

"Cash?"

As if there was a choice? Alan smiled, deciding it must be a joke and he'd play along until he talked to Lydia, get her to call off this dog. "Redneck, let me explain a few things to you about not getting caught."

That evening with Lydia, they made love in the leather recliner in the front room. Alan sat bareass naked, on the verge of sliding off as he held Lydia around the waist on his lap. The prosthetics were off and he had control but moved her like she asked, lifting her up and down on his cock.

"Faster, faster, waitwaitwait, now, start slow."

She told him it felt like she was tied up, helpless in a strange way. It was magic to have a guy *be* her movement.

He slid down in the seat as he felt himself begin to cum, exploding inside Lydia while he choked out grunts and half her name. She rocked her head side to side and took loud breaths. And then it was over. Alan circled his arms around her as she kissed his shoulder. After a while he carried her to the shower, cleaned her body and washed her hair before reconnecting the limbs, wrapping Lydia in a silk robe, and setting her back in her wheelchair. Before he got dressed, he sprayed Lysol on the recliner and wiped it off with a towel.

"I met this weird guy today at the casino, Sweetie. Like, he knew all about the thing with Ronnie and Cap. He tried to hire me like a hit man."

"Was it Norm Fagen?"

Alan shrugged. "He didn't give me a real name."

She blew into her straw and rolled closer. "You guys and your paranoia. He had glasses? Goofy half-long hair, half-bald?"

"That's him. You know him? You told him all the details? I thought we said those were secrets."

"Shit on that. You're a better man than this guy, and I talked you up so nice. He was shaking when he left, wanted *me* to make the call so he wouldn't have to face you head on. I told him you're a real intimidator."

"Why'd you do that? Jesus, I'm not a killer."

"You could be. You handled the Cap and Ronnie thing so well, I think it's a move up in the world for you. Do you want to be small time forever, taking grunt jobs from assholes? Think about the respect."

"Think about the death penalty." *She's out of her mind.*

"It's not like I'm saying be a hit man, Alan. Here's the deal. Norm doesn't know about you and me, this part of it. I told him you work for me mostly, still need your fee. Once the partner is out of the way, Norm needs someone else on board to help with the operation. Someone smarter than this boob. Like, well, me."

"You're talking about dope, aren't you? This is a redneck meth guy, and you're going to hook up with that?"

"Jesus, honey, not like I haven't before. How do you think Ronnie made his money? How do you think I've been able to afford all this plus the gizmos?" Lydia moaned like she was touching herself. "We moved a *lot* of snow back then, man. I'll never be able to spend all this money. Never had anyone on to us, either."

Alan couldn't look at her. His last few weeks with Lydia were amazing for him. She challenged him to look inside and ask if he was satisfied with the man he saw there. Like therapy, almost. She pushed him to be a stronger man, physically and mentally, and worked to break down his comfortable loafer mentality. Here he was thinking she was pushing him towards a good honest living when instead she wanted him to have bigger balls so he could kill people. At that moment, on his knees, naked with Lysol and a towel, he wondered if she tore down the old façade simply to build a new one for him.

She finally said, "Would I do that to you? I've got the money, the connections, friends. Kill one scumbag, that's the target. Skimming dope money to fund bigger dope deals? Come on. We can turn it into a real business, not a free for all."

Alan nodded.

Lydia puffed, rolled the chair closer, her rubber toes touching Alan's love handle.

"I mean, are you really going to play quarter poker as a career?" she said.

Alan shook his head. "How well do you know this Norm guy, anyway?"

"What's this about?" Lydia laughed. "You're jealous? Oh, really, Mr. Crabtree, please. Does he look like my type?"

Alan thought, *If I'm your type...*

"I mean, do you trust him? How long have you known him?"

Lydia's smile was pure tease. "Since high school, at least twelve years. And he's always been ugly. He was a band geek who started a little side business, okay? I used to buy from him, way back then. Smoked a little. The thing is, he's no one. He's hardly made any moves in the world since then, which is why I thought we could trust him."

"You were a band geek?"

The smile disappeared. "I was a *musician*. First chair tenor sax. Norm was a snare drummer."

"I didn't mean anything."

"You should have heard me play."

Alan put his hand on her fake thigh and rubbed softly. It was something he'd discovered early on, when Lydia would have phantom pains and ask him to itch the prosthetics. It seemed to help. Alan wondered if the reverse was true and tried tickling, affectionate touching. As long as she could see it, Lydia swore she felt the tingling.

"I can imagine you were good," Alan said. He looked up at Lydia, who held onto a loose grin while she watched his hand. He made the strokes longer, reaching where the leg attached, not ready to go past it yet.

"That's so nice. You're sweet, Alan."

"Really, though. Nothing between you and Norm?"

"Again with the jealousy? I'm not sure what to say."

"Not even once?" Alan moved his other hand to her other leg, synchronized the rubs as his fingers lingered higher each time. Lydia's breathing grew rougher, half-moans. Alan was getting hard again.

"Jesus, okay. There was once. You want to know?"

"Sure," he said.

"In the drum closet, and I was high, horny, same as Norm, and I blew him a little. God, we were sixteen. Then he pulled my shorts down, took me from behind while I held onto the bass drum. Look, stop the rubbing and get to it."

Alan slipped his fingers inside her and the moans took off like fireworks. The doubts he felt eased for the moment. It was all talk at the moment. When it came to action, Alan was sure he could talk her out of the idea. Kill off a drug dealer? She was a better woman than that.

I hope.

He flicked a couple switches on the chair to make it manual and pushed it backwards to her bedroom. He took the false limbs off and placed her on the bed.

Before he turned her onto her stomach, Lydia said, "Remember to get the snorkel. Just in case I need it."

FOUR

The dye-job on Lancaster only made him more conspicuous. The face didn't match blond at all, and he hadn't smiled much since. Terry thought it was a bad sign and hoped panic wasn't showing through his cool veneer as he tried to paste together a plan. It wasn't so easy. He'd never been involved with murder before.

Terry told him, "It's only until we can get set up out of town."

"Do we really need to leave? It's not like the cops here are all Sam Spade."

"Maybe, but they get better when a cop dies."

They spent the afternoon in a couple neighborhoods, knocking doors to raise pocket money, still came up zero after three hours. Lancaster was getting restless, mumbling and growling under his breath, Terry hearing words like *bank* and *carjack*.

"Look," Terry said. "So many people owe money, credit out the ass, so we'll find something. Cool out a little."

"I'll give you another hour."

"What's got into you?"

Lancaster flashed coffee-stained teeth. "If you don't use them muscles, the muscles wither away. We can storm a little bank, pistol whip the guards, load up and get the hell out. Fifty-nine more minutes, then we do it my way."

Terry let it go, figuring he'd talk his partner down if they didn't score in half an hour. At the next house, he opened the curbside mailbox and sorted through the letters, copied the name *Gibbs* onto his clipboard. They headed up the walk to the front door and rang the bell.

Mr. Gibbs opened the front door to find two overgrown white frat boys on the step. The ball caps, the two-day fuzz on their chins, but they looked at least thirty. Both blond, wearing Dockers and white shirts with cheap ties. Terry had a tweed sport coat and a clipboard, a page on which he flipped before looking up and smiling.

"Mr. Gibbs?" he said.

Gibbs nodded, seemingly wary of salesmen and Gospel pushers. So after the nod, Terry said. "I think you've been expecting us."

"Sorry, no. Unless you're sweepstakes people."

They shared a chuckle.

Terry said, "We're with the collections agency. I'm sure you've gotten a few letters from us already, unanswered, and that's why we're here. You mind if we come in and talk about it?"

Gibbs propped an elbow on the doorjamb and grinned. "So, my CD club sent over a couple of guys to lean on me?"

"Pretty much. Step back, please."

When the man didn't budge, Lancaster raised his hand and pressed Gibbs firmly on the chest, sending him back a foot. He wore a do-nothing expression, hands at his sides. Messy hair and glasses halfway down his nose. Terry followed them in and closed the door. He locked the deadbolt.

"Let's sit down," Terry said. He peeked in doors and found the dining room. "In here."

A bright room, a china cabinet against the wall, an oval table centered, white lace tablecloth with an empty candle holder, a stack of napkins, and tall glass salt and pepper shakers. Terry yanked an end chair, tall-backed with handles, and sat down, crossing his ankles. Lancaster wandered off.

"Where's he going?" Gibbs said.

"Checking. We don't want any dirty surprises. What, are you sick today?"

"No, I'm fine."

"You're in the robe, at home in the middle of the day. Don't you work?"

Gibbs crossed his arms. "I thought you knew all about me."

Terry sighed. He closed his eyes and rubbed his temple up and down with itching fingertips. "Look, they give me a name, an address, and an amount. That's all. I'm trying to make this easy for both of us."

"It's not all that much, really. Two-ten and some change?"

Terry scanned the clipboard, gaze following a finger. "I've got three-fifty."

"No, that's way overboard. You know how it is with these clubs, right? After a while, you forget, they send the wrong stuff, it's a hassle to send it back, and then they forget about you."

"Mr. Gibbs, I know *exactly* how it is, which is why I never join them." Terry pulled a pinkie across his throat while gritting his teeth. "Serious shit. Now, what's with you not working?"

"I'm working at home. I have a book due next week."

"What type of book?"

"A science textbook for high school. I used to teach, now I write textbooks and give lectures to other science teachers."

Terry looked at Gibbs like, *Really? That's just weird.*

Lancaster strolled through, hands in pockets, bored shrug as he went out the opposite door. Gibbs turned in his chair and watched, then said, "I don't want him going in there. That's my study." Gibbs stood and followed before Terry could stop him.

The study was hardwood floor and rugs, wall-to-wall bookcases, one with awards and certificates instead of books. The desk was a long old wooden table. A notebook computer on top, opened, with an aquarium screensaver bubbling, surrounded by stacks of paper and books. Lancaster was browsing bookshelves.

"See anything you like?" Gibbs said.

Lancaster pointed to a high shelf. "*Catch-22* was good. But not *Origin of Species*. Nice concept, bad writer."

Terry came into the study behind Gibbs, held the man by the shoulder. "He's examining the scene. We have to plan these things, you know. It takes hitting the right nerve in order to make you admit you should pay us."

"Look, this is illegal. I've got some friends I could call."

Lancaster turned his head to Gibbs. "You shouldn't have said that. It sounds like a threat." Then he went back to looking at book spines.

Gibbs slipped from under Terry's hand and crossed to his desk. He fingered the touchpad, which brought up his word processor screen, half filled. He palmed the desk wide and hung there, tired like he had run a marathon.

"Here I am, halfway through a chapter on energy, describing inertia, when I get you two come looking for money. Because I didn't pay my CD club. Ridiculous."

"Everybody has a job to do. Some jobs make more global sense, see? Like what you do, or firemen, or nurses. Others fill in little niches. Think about tax lawyers and middle managers and guys who fix roller skates. And then what we do, because bills have to get paid. They just do. That's something economic," Terry said.

Gibbs turned around. Lancaster stopped looking at books and was interested in the couch. He lifted the blue cushions for a look under, found nothing. He sat on the couch, but shifted and bounced, reached behind him and pulled out his 9mm. Terry looked at Gibbs expecting fear, maybe confusion, and he got both. Shit, even Terry was uncomfortable—Lancaster had never pulled it out on a job before. Normal people didn't play tough with guns. Normal people did whatever the people with the guns said and hoped they would leave. Terry hoped Lancaster could keep his finger off the trigger this time.

"Look, you can have the CDs back. The order was wrong, and I should have taped the box back up—"

"No, no, no," Terry said. He walked towards Lancaster with his hands out, shaking them. "What are you doing? Put that away."

"It jammed into my back. It was cutting me."

"Put it away," Terry said, not bothering to disguise anything, voice going too high.

Lancaster stood from the couch, holstered the pistol, the glare at Terry not an act. He smiled an apology at Gibbs.

Terry said, "We have to carry for our own protection. We never threaten a client with a gun. I'm sorry if it looked that way. No, real professionals wouldn't sink that low."

"He's got a pool," Lancaster said.

Gibbs adjusted his glasses. "What about the pool?"

"Let's go take a look," Terry said, hand outstretched asking Gibbs to lead. It usually only took a moment or two of innuendo to get a mark to cave by this point. Stand poolside with the guy, run through the situation again with a hand on his shoulder, never actually *say* what could happen otherwise.

They followed Gibbs through the dining room and kitchen, then out the back door. The pool was in-ground, a small rectangle with a low diving plank surrounded by wrought iron patio furniture. A high privacy fence hid similar postage stamp yards on three sides. On the opposite side of the pool, a small tin shed stood on the leftover grass.

"Looks nice. You keep this up well," Terry said.

"How deep?" Lancaster said.

"It's eight feet. Eight feet."

The water was clear so that the tile shimmered and warbled as the sunlight slipped on top. Bright. The weather was early spring comfortable there. No breeze. Lancaster walked around to the diving board. He stood on it and made a few pretend hops. Arcing his arms and all that. Then he said, "Is the shed locked?"

"No."

"What's in there? That where you keep the chlorine and chemicals?"

"Sure. Can we go back inside now? I'm busy. My wife will be home soon. I promise. Tell your company that I'll pay tomorrow."

"But you won't pay," Terry said.

"Yeah, I will."

"No. As soon as we leave, you get brave again. Saying, 'Screw this, I'm not paying a *dime*,' and firing off a letter to get them off your back." Terry wanted him to cave *so bad* before it went further. "I've seen it a hundred times."

"You morons never pay," Lancaster shouted. He was bumping around in the shed. Terry imagined he might come out with a chainsaw.

Birds chirped. It was a nice day regardless. Gibbs sweated in his heavy robe, be it the heat or the pressure, probably both. Lancaster came out of the shed with a bucket of chlorine and a bottle of PH stuff. Terry gripped Gibbs' shoulder like a father-in-law does a son-in-law. They walked to meet Lancaster at poolside as he untwisted the cap off the PH bottle and then let the whole thing drain into the pool.

"Hey, that screws up the water!" Gibbs said.

"Exactly."

"This doesn't make me want to pay. It gets me mad."

"Not for long. Mr. Lancaster, let's proceed," Terry said.

Lancaster kicked the bucket over so that the chlorine powder lumped into the pool and sizzled and swirled, milky white currents. Gibbs hissed. Terry was ready to pour on the final spiel, wear the man down with a few more sentences. Before he could, Lancaster kneed Gibbs from behind, forcing him to his knees, then grabbed his arms, bent them back, holding the man's head inches above the water. His feet kicked and they nearly lost balance but held on. Terry reached out to Lancaster, got a bad vibe from dark eyes, so he retreated to the wooden fence.

"It'll burn your face, your eyes, maybe your hands, your lungs if you suck any water in," Lancaster said.

"Don't do this, please."

"Come on, man, we *have* to do it. You know that."

Gibbs caught the fumes in his nose and mouth and coughed like he had TB. Hacking and wheezing at poolside with a frat boy thug hovering over him. Terry peeked through the slats to see if the neighbors were listening. *What if Lancaster kills him anyway? We get some pocket change, but then he comes right back out and holds him under?*

"Oh Jesus oh Jesus I'll pay you okay? Oh Jesus I'll pay you."

"Yeah, you will."

He coughed more, caught his breath, had that "about to vomit" cough going. Then he said, "I'll get my checkbook and pay you—"

"No check."

"No check? They always want checks."

"They've run out of patience with you. You can give us a check and then stop payment. Or it could bounce. And if they get mad a second time, it won't be this easy next trip," Lancaster said.

"I promise, it'll be a good check."

"Bad answer? Ready to dunk?"

"Come on, man," Terry said. He crawled to Gibbs' side and whispered, "I'm trying to help you here. This guy's serious."

Lancaster nodded. "I'll sing, too. Won't pull him up until I get through all of 'Boot Scoot Boogie.'"

"No, no," Gibbs said. Pathetic little girl whine.

Lancaster pulled him up and let go. Gibbs scuttled back and crossed his arms.

"Okay, fine! Cash! I'll give you cash!"

They waited for Gibbs to get to his feet, then followed him into the study. He looked through his wallet.

"Three fifty," Lancaster said, completely in charge. Terry hung out in the dining room, not wanting to watch the rest of this.

"That's too much."

"Interest and expenses. Three fifty, you bastard."

Gibbs pulled out a hundred and twenty-four dollars, handed the cash over. He said the rest was in his bedroom. Lancaster followed Gibbs to the bedroom, where he looked through drawers, and then looked through his wife's bedside hutch. He pulled out her secret money stash and counted out two hundred twenty, then shook his head.

"No ones or fives. Sorry."

Terry and Lancaster made eye contact a moment. Lancaster said, "Cut him a break?"

"I'm feeling a little embarrassed about this anyway. Usually we don't have to go so far. Sure. A six dollar break." Terry nodded at Gibbs, reached out for the money. He folded it and stuck it in his coat pocket.

On the way out, Terry grabbed his clipboard. He apologized quietly to Gibbs, then said, "If they send you more letters, pay again anyway, okay? Don't remind them about us, because we're not supposed to exist. Like black ops. They'll deny everything. So it might end up costing more than you thought."

Gibbs didn't say anything. He stared at the floor and shivered.

Lancaster opened the door. They walked through, Terry calling back, "Good luck on the book" before closing it.

Outside on the sidewalk, Terry and Lancaster headed for their car. It was parked a few blocks away, near where they'd started the rounds earlier looking for a sucker.

Terry split the money, handed Lancaster his share.

"I can't believe it. Not bad," Lancaster said.

"I told you. He was about to break, though. You didn't have to go so far."

"That wasn't so far. He's not even bruised. Only thing is he's got a fucked-up pool."

Terry shook his head, watched the sidewalk, feelings of junior high returning. He was good friends with the bully as long as he didn't criticize. A little sarcasm cost him a chokehold behind the band hall one afternoon. Hurt like a mother. Before the past few days, he didn't think Lancaster would hurt him. Now, it was more like fifty-fifty.

"Think he'll tell?" Lancaster said.

"Probably. Nobody will believe him at first. He can't prove we weren't who we said we were. And the descriptions? Lose the hat and shave, whole new face. Bingo."

They got to the car. Lancaster dropped into the driver's seat, and Terry settled into the passenger side. The engine started and they pulled away. He cranked the classic rock station. Mountain's 'Mississippi Queen.'

Lancaster said, "You were right, though. The good thing about America. Everybody's in debt."

FIVE

The cowboy Norm gave Alan the name and address of his thieving partner and half the three grand upfront. Lydia had laughed at him when he asked if she was really going through with it. She said she had some old untraceable guns in the garage, Ronnie's emergency stash, and told him to take what he needed. So Alan kept playing. He supposed if he wanted, nothing was really holding him to Lydia other than good sex and easy money, but he was beginning to feel like a lap dog.

He took a drive over to the mark's house, parked on the curb, and decided to learn the guy's routine. After a couple days, Alan didn't think there *was* a routine. The guy hadn't left the house. Alan spent most of the time glancing over some horse racing magazines—*Daily Racing Forum* and *Mid-Atlantic Thoroughbred*—and eating chicken nuggets from Wendy's.

The mark's name was Randy Tompkins. He came outside to get the mail and the paper dressed in indecent shorts and flip-flops. Wild-assed frizzy hair, probably liked it that way. He had one visitor, a short woman who could've been in high school (or mistaken for it), bright blonde with heavy make-up. She came by, stayed a while, and when she left, lingered at the door for long embarrassing kisses. She scratched her legs a lot.

Lydia rang Alan's cell phone. "You done yet?"

"Soon. I thought I could get him while he was out, but he doesn't leave."

"Then just go in there."

"I've been here long enough to be noticed. How about I borrow a different car and come back tonight?"

Lydia was quiet. Alan thought he heard music over the line—*McCartney and Wings?* And then a faint voice.

"Have you got company, Sweetie?"

"No, no one here." Too quick. Alan started thinking he was right about her and Norm. Her story about him was hot, yeah, though Alan felt a little pissed afterward. Lydia made him feel better, though. She said he had the animal in him while Norm had been a fumbling kid. It could've been a smokescreen, though. Maybe she was ready to give the grown-up Norm a second chance.

"I'll come over for lunch," Alan said.

"Sure. Bring Mexican."

He turned off the phone and looked up, surprised to see Tompkins on the sidewalk, still goofy and half-naked, standing with arms crossed, a heavy stare aimed at Alan.

Shit, Alan thought. He was careless for a minute and the guy spotted him. Under the dumb exterior, Tompkins was still a successful drug pusher, one who hadn't been caught or snitched out. Successful enough that his own partner wanted him out of the way. Alan was impressed before remembering he didn't really want to go through with this.

He let the window down and motioned for Tompkins to come over. Tompkins eased closer, arms still crossed, bending at the waist for a better look.

"I'm a little lost," Alan said. "I was looking for a green Volkswagen. Some guy on this street was selling it, I think. You seen one?"

Tompkins shifted his look from Alan to the Monte Carlo. "This car's nice enough."

"The bug's for my daughter."

Tompkins nodded and Alan waited, thinking the guy would say he hadn't seen one, maybe try a different street. Instead, "Bullshit."

"Excuse me?" Alan said.

"I'm saying you've been parked out here a long damn time, and you were here yesterday, too. I should have said something then."

Alan wanted to crank up and go, get out of sight before Tompkins could get the plate number, a fake registered to an address in Alabama, courtesy of Terry and Lancaster. If he ran, though, the gig was over and no telling how Lydia would react. She trusted him to pull it off, so Alan said, "Maybe you'd better get in."

Tompkins laughed and shook his head, got louder and louder.

Alan pulled out his fake ATF shield, something he'd picked up to help him get away from odd jobs gone bad before he met Lydia. Any drops, spoiler trips, or messenger runs went south, the shield bought five or ten minutes to make some distance between him and the scene. He flashed it at Tompkins.

"Mr. Tompkins, I'm here to save your life."

Five minutes in the car and Tompkins was convinced that his partner had tried to hire a hit man, but hired "Special Agent Mitchell" instead—Alan helping keep Tompkins alive until it was time for money to be exchanged.

"We then would have approached you about faking him out. You've seen that before? We stage you like a corpse at a crime scene, take some pictures. As soon as the final payment is in hand, *bam*, he goes to jail."

"Why not arrest him now?"

Alan clicked his tongue. "You don't want it thrown out of court, do you?"

Tompkins nodded like he understood. Alan hoped he could do this quickly, since the guy smelled awful. Thick musk. Alan wondered if pheromones attracted the high school girl more than Tompkins' ugly ass looks.

"You pretend like you don't know anything, and it'll go smoothly. Believe me, nothing will happen in the meantime. Stick to the plan and put on a good act in front of Norm until I contact you again."

Tompkins pushed the door open, then stopped with a foot out and a foot in. "Wait, aren't you going to still keep watch on me? You know, in case of an emergency?"

Alan smiled, shifted the car into gear so the guy would get a clue. He said, "We'll be around. If you don't see us so easily, know we're always here for you. Whatever it was that got this guy mad at you, maybe it's a good day to swear off it. Make it like Lent or something."

Tompkins nodded and said a lot of things that almost sounded like "Thanks" as he climbed out and shut the door gently. Alan saluted him and took off. Down the road, he tried to fill in the rest of the plan since that first part was off the top of his head. The idea was to string Tompkins' along a while, maybe get some money out of him without actually having to kill the guy. If Tompkins and Norm confronted each other over this, Alan guessed he wouldn't need to kill anyone. Let those two settle it face to face while he took Lydia on a cruise or something.

Enough of that crap. Get some Mexican takeout, spend some time with Lydia. He wanted to smell her, a close examination, to check if Norm had been with her or not. Either way, Alan thought his plan was the better option, just in case. Get paid, let these morons clean up their own end of the gene pool, and keep Lydia all to himself—until the next guy shows up making big ass mistakes trying to fuck his girl.

After the agent pulled away, Tompkins glanced at surrounding houses and parked cars, covered boats and backyard tool sheds, wondering where the ATF guys hid to watch him. Why would ATF care anyway, unless they already knew about his business? Shit, with Winona hanging around like she did, both for sex and as a courier, how could they not? Probably waiting until after they stopped the assassin to bust Tompkins for the dope. That last thing the agent said, like a warning: *I'd swear off it.* Man, yeah, they knew.

Tompkins walked back inside the house while he did some math in his head—*how many months until Winona's eighteenth birthday? Fourteen?* He was sunk all over. He knew Norm wasn't happy with the expansion project, but hiring a hit man? *Damn!* If Tompkins had told him up-front, "Okay, no problem. We'll keep it down low," then he'd be clear. Now he was sweating and shaking. He dropped onto his couch stared at the big screen TV, a *Saturday Night Live* rerun on cable.

He thought, *What if the agents came knocking, happened to look around the house, and found the stash?* Winona could bring some friends over and sneak the stuff out to a safe place. *But what if the agents had super-telescopic lenses and ultraviolet cameras?* They'd see him having buck wild sex with a sixteen-year-old high school dropout. Damn, how she fucked like a college girl, like she'd try anything and pretty much already had.

He looked at the wet spot on his shorts, then closed his eyes and banged his head against the back of the couch. He couldn't trust the Feds, couldn't trust Norm, so he was screwed. Unless he hired his own guys, found another way out of this shit.

He found an address book in the kitchen in the pantry where he kept most of his plastic baggies and tin foil. A secret compartment behind that was full of ecstasy and pot. He flipped through the book while leaning against the sink, then remembered the window over the sink and ducked down, sat on the floor.

A couple of guys he used to work with. Lately, they'd been dealing in hot cars they picked up on the side of the interstate. If the money was right, Terry and Lancaster handled almost anything. Tompkins found the listing. He'd already scratched out six numbers for them over the years and hoped the most recent still worked. He crawled across the sticky kitchen tiles to the bedroom, found his wireless tangled in the sheets he and Winona had kicked off the bed, and tried the number.

SIX

Both blond, both sleepy, Terry and Lancaster sat propped against the wall in their booth at Ruby Tuesdays shaking their heads at Tompkins and his dumb-ass offer. Terry tapped Lancaster's arm and gave him a squinty-eyed head weave and grin. Tompkins was asking them to kill his business partner, who hired someone first to kill Tompkins. Tit for tat. He had no idea how ridiculous it sounded. Terry and Lancaster couldn't blame him, though.

Terry said, "We've got to leave now."

Tompkins raised a hand, almost waved it in Terry's face.

"I can pay more," he said.

Lancaster said. "You like my hair?"

"What, you dyed it? Or the black was dye. I don't notice those things."

"We're changing our image, maybe going into a different type of business. We don't have time for this crap." Lancaster sipped his iced tea.

Tompkins went dumb-faced. "Aren't you guys my friends? Come on, Terry. What did I ever do to you guys except help out?"

Terry slid closer to Tompkins, held a hand over his mouth and mumbled, "Friends would've noticed my partner's new hair, would've taken a hint. No friend, you."

"Why'd you even come, then?"

"We're curious, I guess. Looking for something safer, thought you might have a lead. Seems we were mistaken."

Lancaster said, "Don't you and this Norm guy work among the kiddies?"

"The X? Not much anymore. The local cops are shutting down everyone they can find, giving in to politics. I was going to let that part slide. The kids don't care where they get it anyway. I doubt one of them can describe my face if pressed." He left out his plan about moving into heroin and cocaine, a step up in the world cash-wise, a more sophisticated clientele, not to mention a safer business all around.

"That's too bad, because we've never been much for the killing game," Terry said. It was as much a hint to Lancaster as it was an answer to Tompkins.

Lancaster nodded, not as good as keeping a poker face as Terry. "Nearly retired. At least for a while. Like a Michael Jordan retirement, what other people call a vacation."

"What if someone kills me, then? Or even if this Fed agent stops him, I'm still tied up, right? I'll owe them. If you step in on my side, you'll have all the work you want, or you'll be left alone. Otherwise..."

Terry nodded slowly. Lancaster watched him, no emotional response or reflex. Tompkins must have thought they were the perfect team—impossible to read from the outside, but in seemingly telepathic sync with each other. A pretty good con, same as everything else they did. Terry was having trouble sleeping at night in the condo, not so much at the memories of the past few days—the dead trooper, the textbook writer and his pool—but more from fear Lancaster might do something he couldn't talk them out of. Then it was life in prison or a needle in the arm ending everything. Worse came to worse, a shot in the face from his own partner.

They needed cash, though. It wouldn't hurt to get some walking-around money and then later ditch Tompkins, the Coast, all of it.

"How much you offering?" Terry asked.

"Three thousand."

"Up front?"

Tompkins shook his head. "A deal like this, I need to attend the funeral. I say maybe twelve hundred now, the rest later."

"Why twelve hundred?" Lancaster said.

"That's what I've got in the car. Probably more like twelve-oh-three and seventy cents, so let's round down."

Terry said, "Might as well take the change. We might want to grab a couple Cokes out of a machine."

"No problem."

"You've got a picture of your partner? So we can be sure. And tell us about this agent in case we run into him."

"No. You can't miss this agent, man. He's pretty bulky, pretty short. Probably wouldn't be a bad looking guy if he lost most of the weight. His car's goddamned nice, I tell you."

Lancaster scrunched his eyebrows. "Yeah?"

"A Monte Carlo, black, almost brand new."

Terry and Lancaster fought to keep from laughing. They made faces at each other. *It can't be...*

"What about him? You know him?"

Terry shook his head. "Sounds like a nice car, though." He rose from his bench and said, "I've got to piss."

Lancaster scooted to the end, pushing Tompkins out of the way.

Tompkins watched these two head to the restroom together.

Lancaster washed his hands for no real reason other than keeping occupied while Terry whizzed. Alone in the restroom, they still whispered at each other.

Terry said, "All this time, that cell phone number was still on. I shouldn't have even answered. I can't believe I forgot to lose it. Shit."

"What do you think, though? It's got to be Crabtree. What's he up to?"

"Half a ton? Maybe you didn't hear Randy clearly. It involves kill—" Terry cut himself off, started up with, "Involves something we shouldn't do any more of, right?"

"Hell, it's not like we did a bad job the first time. Plus we know the target is a soft touch."

Terry shook himself, zipped up, and finished reading baseball scores on the *USA Today* sports page framed above the urinal. Starting to think Lancaster was bat-shit insane, some blown fuse in his head. Maybe a tumor. Finally, he turned, shoved his hands in his pockets, and stretched his neck.

He said, "What if we say yes, take half up-front, *warn* the partner, then turn them all in? We're like Brutus to Caesar. We get paid, Randy and his buddy get nailed, Crabtree gets screwed over, and then we leave town."

Lancaster elbowed the dryer button, methodically rubbed every inch of his hands, even between his fingers. He said, "That's a bullshit deal. We don't squeal. I say we take a look at the bigger picture—get rid of both and find their dope. We can be players that way."

Terry shrugged, tried to sound on the fence instead of dead opposed. "Sounds risky. Let's give it some thought."

He reached for the door.

"You aren't going to wash up?" Lancaster said.

SEVEN

Alan sat on Lydia's couch because Norm was in the leather chair. He hated someone else sitting in his chair, considering all the sweat he'd wiped off it after making love to Lydia. He felt like a pit bull marking his territory, growling at other dogs. This one kept coming anyway. Norm slumped low in the chair with his knees wide. He was here to tell Lydia a little more about the operation, get her thinking of a new business model. Alan wished he would hurry and leave, stop the chit-chat. Lydia probably knew that, too, so she kept up the small talk and offered him a beer. Now he and Lydia had been talking a good ten minutes.

It was all about people Alan didn't even know. The whole time, he couldn't shake images of a sixteen-year-old fully limbed Lydia being fed Norm's meat in a band closet. New images popped up like animated web ads—Lydia fucking Norm on *his* recliner, Norm gently cleaning her afterwards. He knew it hadn't happened, since he checked thoroughly the day before when he stopped by with lunch. The shampoo bottles and soap were dry, still in place. No mysterious wads of tissue in the trash. No evidence at all. Maybe he imagined the background voice on the phone.

A voice grumbled low in Alan's head: *That doesn't mean anything. Maybe he just fingered her, ate her pussy. Maybe she sucked him off. All sorts of possibilities.*

This guy wouldn't take care of her, clean her up, feed her, dress her, all the things Alan loved to do because she seemed to like the way he did them. Shoulder rubs, doing her make-up, washing her hair. Norm had no clue what it took. Sex with Lydia was one thing, but *loving* her meant sacrifice. Norm wasn't even able to sacrifice his goofy mullet hair even though all the signs screamed *Let it go, man.*

Finally, the conversation lapsed into half-sentences, awkward pauses. Lydia sipped her straw and backed up. Alan stood, escorted Norm to the front door. He tried to shake Alan's hand.

"Please, I'm not a hand shaker. Hope you understand," Alan said.

Norm grinned. "I can't make you like me, can I? Can't buy you a few beers?"

"I like my business life separated from everything else. Makes things easier, no room for confusion."

"Confusion?"

Alan nodded and raised his eyebrows. "If business and friendship were to mix, it wouldn't be long before my friends become the object of my business. You get me?"

He thought Norm paled a little. Maybe it was a cloud moving over the sun. The expression was priceless, though. Like a groom when the preacher asks if he'll take this woman to be his wife—the split second of realization that if he ever fucks someone different, it'll cost him.

Norm climbed into his truck without another word. Alan closed the front door and eased back into the living room, trying to cool down his agitation, avoid a fight with Lydia. It was too late.

"Maybe you could *not* antagonize my new employee, Sweetie."

He looked at the floor to avoid the flaming eyes and marble face. "If I'm supposed to be your enforcer, I have to be pretty harsh."

"You are an enforcer. For me. But, Jesus, you can't run off business. Especially from friends."

"Whoa, now. Not my friend." Alan found some nerve and stared her down, stabbed a finger in the air. "This is your guy, your childhood sweetheart. I think he fell out of a tree. To you, he's gold. Don't give me that 'our friend' shit, because if it were up to me, I'd tie him to a pole somewhere and pray for lightning."

Lydia laughed. She did that sometimes when she was angry. Laughed at him like he'd said the dumbest thing in the world. If it was supposed to make him feel small, then job well done.

Alan scratched the back of his neck while she sputtered, mocking him. He worried that fights like this would end the relationship, and was always surprised when she got turned on by their arguments, which happened more than he thought was healthy. He'd learned to read her and knew this wasn't one of those times. It lacked the far more vicious sarcasm that made her tingle, and in this case, it was about another guy. Alan wanted to kick the couch until either the wood frame or his foot broke.

"If he were smart," Lydia said, "then we'd be in deep trouble. The reason I don't mind working with Norm is because he *is* infatuated with me and isn't too quick to see that I'll run the show in no time. Yes, I know it and I'm using it to our advantage."

She puffed her straw and rolled closer to Alan.

"Rub my head."

Alan did, almost reflexively. His fingers wove through her soft hair and gently kneaded her scalp. This always calmed her down, made her feel less helpless, so she told him. It had the opposite effect, Alan falling under a spell whenever he touched her, Lydia able to get anything she asked for.

"Mmmm, that's nice," she said. "Don't let this get to you. Norm's a fuck up. You're the one I want, sweetie. You're my true partner in all of this."

He kept rubbing while staring out a far window. What Lydia said made him feel pretty good, even if he didn't believe it one bit.

EIGHT

Alan watched the house from farther away this time, using strong binoculars. He was in a rental car, a top model Kia. Not bad, but not his style. He thought Tompkins was alone that day. No visitors all morning, no one leaving either. Alan saw an occasional shadow behind a curtain, nothing more.

Lydia expected today to be the day, so Alan needed to make some sort of effort, like it or not. Half-thoughts drifted through his head about actually going through with the job, and he read a few hit man books in his spare time—a bunch of *Executioner* novels, militia how-to guides—just in case. The best place to kill Tompkins was probably his own house, make it look like a break-in. Better if he had a bag of "Norm DNA" to sprinkle all over.

Still, at home there would be neighbors, bored enough to come looking if they heard something confusing. If not in the house, then far out in woods or on the Gulf. Alan didn't have a boat, and neither did Lydia or her dead ex-husband. So this needed to be a trip north of I-10 to the pine forest that covered so much of the state. Small towns were cut out here and there, as well as highways and timber mills, although for the most part, the woods were untouched except by wildlife and hunters.

He didn't plan to use it, but Alan chose a hefty .45 from the stash in Lydia's garage. It looked cheap and old. A nice trip to the woods, a shot in the head, a shallow grave, then collect the rest of his money.

No, no, no. Then Lydia and Norm will turn on you and you'll go to jail for a long goddamn time. Paranoia and fear, hand in hand, the only things he felt lately when he wasn't plowing away at Lydia, hoping the animal need was what love really felt like. He had no idea. He pushed it out of his mind and thought, *Take him to the woods, tell him the score, and hope he takes the advice to get lost. So as far as they'll know, I killed him.*

Alan cranked the Kia and took a block before pulling into Tompkins' driveway.

Terry and Lancaster were having a hard time watching Alan Crabtree watching Tompkins. They kept cracking up thinking about the fat bastard bluffing as a Fed, trying to run a scam on a basically harmless drug pusher. Maybe Norm was the one who hired him in the first place. With Crabtree involved, the death threat probably wasn't real anyway.

"*Crabtree?*" Terry said, slapping the steering wheel of the minivan they'd found near Slidell under an overpass. He'd said it five or six times, always sending Lancaster into spasms of giggling. "Jesus."

"I like slapping him around. It's fun."

"Yeah. Too bad he paid the car off. We should think up surcharges."

After pulling into Tompkins' driveway, Crabtree had gone to the door and disappeared inside. A few minutes later he reemerged with Tompkins trailing. The guy looked more sleepy than usual, wearing surfer shorts and a faded Sea Wolves T-shirt that was stretched tight. *Probably belonged to the teenager he was fucking*, Lancaster thought. *Lucky guy.*

Terry laughed. "Sea Wolves. Ice hockey in Mississippi. I can't believe anyone fell for that."

"There's another team in Jackson, one in Lafayette. It's like a snow cone on a hot day."

Crabtree climbed into the rented Kia. Tompkins shuffled to the other side, lifted the handle before Alan hit the auto-unlock. He did it three more times until Crabtree pantomimed *Wait until I do this...*

"How sure are we there's not a camera crew around? Crabtree's a walking comedy act. Like that mailman from Seinfeld."

"Newman was evil."

"No, just an asshole who *thought* he was evil. He never pulled it off entirely."

Against all odds, Tompkins figured out how to open the door and seat himself. Crabtree eased from the driveway and drove out of the neighborhood.

Terry shifted into gear and followed slowly, hoping Alan hadn't magically grown wiser since their last meeting, when the fat man laid six hundred in Terry's hand, grinned at their shocked faces, and left without a word. They had been prepared to listen to another sob story, slap him around, take his wallet, and repo the stolen car. Instead, they got paid. It was a disappointment.

"So, should we stop him now before he gets bold and kills Tompkins?" Lancaster said.

Terry barked laughter, feeling back in control for a change, thumping the wheel in rhythms like on old Santana albums. He thought of Carlos in the sixties, big fro, psychedelic swirls painted on the guitar. "Bold? Bold ain't the word, amigo. Alan Crabtree is the antithesis of boldness."

Alan drove north on Highway Fifteen on the twisty two-lane road leading into deep woods. The homes were built in little clusters miles apart. A few farming areas, or people who pretended to be farmers. Cows and horses scattered near dilapidated wooden fences. He listened to talk radio out of New Orleans the first ten minutes, thinking Tompkins was either stoned or mute. The man barely said two words since Alan explained that they needed to meet with other agents discuss a plan for catching Norm and his hired killers. He didn't question it or anything.

Then Tompkins began babbling. Alan had to talk back, and he didn't like that as much as the silence.

"If I haven't told you already, I appreciate your help," Tompkins said. "I'm surprised anyone cares about me enough to protect me this way."

"It's my job."

"You seem to take personal interest. I'm not just a job to you. I'm a real human being. Right? I can tell. You watching my house and all, trying to stay out of sight. I get it now. Like a guardian angel."

Alan remembered some of a hit man guidebook, this underground thing he'd found cheap on E-bay: *Don't get attached. While you may sometimes have to open up, express your emotions, as well as pretend to care about your target's emotions, too, remember that it's acting, a job, like an eight hour shift for a telemarketer. Do the work, take the good with the bad, wash it off, and move on.*

What a dumb-ass writer.

Alan didn't care about Tompkins. He worried his natural fear of pretty much everything might get in the way come crunch time. Shooting Cap had been about survival. Lydia and Norm wanting Tompkins dead was simply about money and power, a hostile takeover of his shares in the company. Maybe that's why it felt different, like he had an unfair advantage by lying to Tompkins, all because someone was paying him. How could mob enforcers and Ninjas live with themselves? What was the secret? Alan hoped he wouldn't have to find out, hoped that Tompkins would take his advice and disappear, change his name, whatever. Give him twenty bucks and point him towards the next town.

Terry and Lancaster hung back far enough that they had to speed up when Alan turned onto a side road without a signal. Panic set in as they reached the dirt path, a cloud of red dust obscuring the view.

"Shit, he might really do it. What's the angle on this? Maybe he's bringing Tompkins to meet the *real* killers, guys with nerve," Lancaster said.

"You heard what he did to Ronnie. I'm starting to think Crabtree graduated from Cowardly Lion stage and moved on to Bad Ass training."

"So if we want our second pay day..."

Terry didn't drive too fast because he couldn't see through the dust. It was a narrow road, probably only used by hunters, or teenagers looking for privacy. As the view cleared, the Kia was almost right in front of them. They braked hard, inches away from the back bumper, their own dust drifting ahead.

"Get your gun," Lancaster said.

"What gun? I didn't bring a gun."

"What the hell?"

A shrug. "It's Crabtree. I didn't think I would need one."

Lancaster pulled out his nine, said, "I'll make sure you don't get any on you."

Alan's life was all about bad timing. He was just through his first try at the truth when he heard the brakes squeal nearby. Hands in his pockets, one curled around a twenty and the other around the pistol grip. Tompkins was shaking the way stoners do when faced with real danger.

"But what about you guys? Feds are on my side, right?" Tompkins said.

Alan shook his head. "You don't get it. There are no feds. Norm wants you dead and if I don't do it, someone else will. I mean it, man. Just find the road, turn left, and keep walking until you hit Wiggins, maybe four or five miles."

He had started to pull the money from his pocket when the brakes echoed, followed by slamming car doors. The distraction spooked Alan and gave Tompkins a little confidence.

"Here! We're over here!"

Rustling bushes. Louder. Faster.

Tompkins got cocky. "Nobody's telling me to leave town, bitch. I'm gonna kick your ass."

"Back down," Alan said, pistol sliding from the pocket of his khakis, slow enough that Tompkins didn't notice.

"Fuck you." Tompkins flashed a spacey grin like he was in a rap video, no longer taking the little fat man seriously.

Alan needed to be taken seriously. He boiled. His grip firmed on the pistol.

Tompkins bobbed, weaved, played like a boxer, took a swipe at Alan and laughed. "I'll lay you out and take your car, man. Here I was thanking you for saving my life."

"I'm trying."

"Playing me for a fool." Another swipe, this one too close.

Alan arm came up, stiffened, Tompkins tripping back to get away.

You run, you won't make it. You give up, could be worse. He worth it to you?

Tompkins was on his knees, shuffling through the dirt and leaves. "Keep cool, man, cool out."

Alan caught a glimpse of two men coming towards them, flickering between trees. He turned back to Tompkins, pulled the trigger.

Terry and Lancaster caught the final moments of Tompkins' life. He stood like he was about to pounce on Crabtree, like it was all a game. Alan straightened his arm, big ass hand cannon. Tompkins went girly on the ground.

Flash, bang, echo, and Tompkins flopped backwards before smacking the ground, blood all over his face down his chest.

"Shit, Crabtree, man, what the fuck?" Lancaster shouted.

Alan came back to earth from whatever place he had gone to make that shot. His face softened from stone cold to shock. He swung the pistol towards Terry and Lancaster, who both tossed up their hands and made soothing sounds.

"Hey, hey," Terry said. "Cool out there, partner. Whatever happened, we're on your side, you know. Didn't we give you a good deal on the car? Weren't we true to our word?"

They took careful steps, drifting apart to split Alan's attention, treating him like a wild boar. He retreated, his gun still up and ready, back and forth. Tompkins' body was in the way, so Alan stepped over it, nearly slipping on the blood. Lancaster jerked forward as if he were reaching to help steady Alan. The fat little man caught the movement and let off a wild shot in Lancaster's direction.

Lancaster went down grabbing his arm, a sharp "Motherfuck!" escaping before he gritted his teeth and hissed, dropped his gun.

Terry backed way off, hands wide, skin going three shades of green. "It's going to be okay, just fine. Calm down, hear me? Easy does it."

The .45 looked bigger to Terry, and it grew larger still as Alan took slow steps straight for him, the eyes no longer scared, the mouth a thin line of control.

"On your stomach," Alan said.

"Alan, buddy—"

"Look at your friend over there. Say another word, see what happens. On your stomach."

Terry inched his body closer to the floor of the woods, trying to keep his eye on the gun in case he needed to move quickly. His cheeks twitched, eyes squinted, not wanting to take a bullet fully aware of it.

"You can't kill us, man. We're connected. They'll find out somehow."

"I paid you in cash."

"Still, there's always a trail. Watch *CSI*. Always something to find the connection. Listen, you let us go, we'll help you out. Nothing to it."

Terry could only turn his neck so far now as he stretched out on the ground, hands on his head. He thought Alan hadn't moved except to lower the gun barrel. Ahead of him, Lancaster rolled on the ground in serious pain, blood slicking his whole right arm.

"I can't trust you," Alan said. Simple fact, no question at all.

"Deal with us here, dude. We'll get rid of the body for you. Something you'd have to do anyway, have you thought about that? I know you don't want to leave him here, right?"

It was exactly what Alan wanted to do. He rethought the plan, wishing he could make the final shots and let it go. Anyone who found these three would think it was a drug deal gone wrong. They were known criminals, while Alan was a nobody, in the clear. Lydia's rich friends thought she was slumming with Alan, using him in a way better looking men wouldn't stand for. A killer? Not likely.

The little bastards on the ground had wounded him enough already. Several beatings over late payments administered by these fraternity rejects. *Go ahead. You're home free.*

Alan mumbled, "I've only been paid for one."

"What?"

"Nothing. Look, you dispose of Tompkins. It'll be your car, your fingerprints, Lancaster's blood, so don't think of trying to turn it back on me."

"Didn't cross my mind."

"They find that body in the next few weeks, I'll know you didn't do a good job, and I'll come find you."

"Got it. Clear as a bell."

Without another word, Alan eased his way down the path he had come from, making his steps quiet so Terry wouldn't know where he was, the guy twisting his neck, his vision blocked by tangled tree roots and vines. Alan kept calm, didn't run the last ten feet. He kept his eyes on the path, made sure he wasn't being followed, then got into his Kia and turned back down the dirt path around Terry and Lancaster's minivan.

He kept thinking he did the stupid thing. Had them right there, easy to end it all. But he wasn't a real killer. In the movies, guys like him turned out okay. It was the bad guys who gave in to emotions and made mistakes. He clicked the radio on and tried to simmer down, but he couldn't. He had killed a helpless stoner, wounded a muscle-bound maniac, and left a con man as a witness.

Shit, Alan thought as sweat chilled his skin. *It's far from over.*

NINE

Lydia saw the potential in Alan despite the homeliness. Yes, he had slimmed down for her, paid closer attention to his hair and clothes, but that didn't solve the pug face and overall stumpy nature. She overlooked that because he tried harder than any man she had ever known. He gave in to her mostly, didn't mind risking a small fight. And the sex was all for her, she could tell. Lydia usually told him what she wanted. The other times she guessed he was reading *Cosmo* on the side and taking it seriously.

Then Norm came back into her life. Rough around the edges, not as much of a pushover. He was more of a take charge guy, though less bright than Alan. Still, she liked the chase, the fighting spirit. She could get him to change his style, maybe shave his head and lose that stupid mullet and ball cap, trim the beard to stubble, dress him in outfits a little more urban. That appealed to her, taming the beast inside Norm so she could hold him on a leash, same as Alan.

The trick was, she knew, having them both in her stable and liking it. Lydia would choose whom she slept with night to night, sometimes indulging in both. Working and playing together, a little family. When she daydreamed about it, the chair wasn't in the picture. Her beautiful arms and legs were whole and attached, true flesh instead of rubber illusions. Lounging in her silk robe on the sofa until her boys came home, guns and cash in hand, another job complete. Meeting them with kisses as they began undressed her, then made love to her simultaneously while wearing their expensive suits. *Yes, more, yes, all for me, for ME—*

The phone jangled her nerves and made her gasp a little, the daydream now a faded second of thought. Lydia tried to lift her arm before remembering it wasn't real anymore, then closed her eyes and whispered, "Answer."

Alan's breath exploded like static on the headset.

"Calm down, I'm here. Alan? Everything go all right?"

"No, it's all screwed. Sweetie, it wasn't my fault."

Sure it wasn't, she thought. "Please calm down and tell me what happened."

He told her, quickly enough that she barely understood—the car thieves had followed him, must've have known about this the whole time. Her first thought flashed Norm in league with these guys, a big play to take her and Alan out of the picture. Maybe blackmail. She held that in check while imagining other scenarios. Could be they had followed Alan from the time he paid them off for the car, curious as to where he got the cash. Or, if not Norm, maybe Tompkins himself had called the little fucks in.

Later. She would find out later. For the moment, there were more important things. "You took care of them, right? Terry and Lancaster?"

"How could I do that? Three bodies instead of one? There's no *way* I could've gotten away with that."

Lydia felt scared. She watched the curtains flowing in the wind, wondering if there were killers outside her home already, waiting for the perfect moment. She was defenseless. They could do anything they wanted to her.

"Come home, Alan. How far away are you?"

"South of Wiggins, so I should be hitting Highway Ninety in about ten minutes."

"Hurry." She hung up and sipped the straw control, spinning slowly to make sure she was alone. Someone was usually around to shut those windows, but the idea that the daytime would be as dangerous as the night never occurred to her before that moment. The pretty sheer curtains, the beige furniture with pastel pillows and throws, her four-post bed, her perfectly sculpted Jayne Mansfield limbs—none of them offered any protection from bastard car thieves or federal agents or *real* assassins for hire, not like her sweet vulnerable Alan.

He was too far away at that moment, still a good half-hour out. She spoke into her mike, dialed Norm's number. He was closer, maybe only a few blocks. Whatever the risk of Norm not playing straight with them on this, Lydia didn't want to be alone.

TEN

Terry didn't move until he was absolutely sure Crabtree was gone. He waited for the sound of the engine turning over before he scuttled towards Lancaster, who wasn't groaning anymore. He lay curled on his side, a bloody mess. The bullet had passed through his bicep, pulped it.

For a moment, Terry imagined running for it. Take the gun. Put Lancaster out of his misery. Drive, drive, drive. Only a split second, because he knew he wouldn't get far without Lancaster. They filled in each other's weak spots.

Besides, Lancaster had already read his friend's mind. "By the time you lift my gun, I'd have found a way to kill you anyway."

"Hey, we're cool, buddy. You need some help."

"Fuck yeah I need help. A *hospital*, man."

Terry let out a deep sigh, trying to think of a better option.

"No, not this time," Lancaster said. "Damn the consequences. We can't do this on our own. You can make up a story, say I was cleaning my gun. Let's get out of here, try for Hattiesburg."

It was a college town about fifty miles north of the Coast, these woods outside of Wiggins the halfway point. If Lancaster wanted a hospital so bad, he must have believed the wound was a life or death choice. He'd never flinched this much the whole time Terry knew him. They could probably get away with a trip to the ER, tell the docs it was an accident.

Terry helped Lancaster to his feet, leaned him against a tree. Then he straddled Tompkins' body, ripped the T-shirt off, and brought it to Lancaster, tied it around the wound.

Lancaster nodded at the body. "What about him? I heard what you told Crabtree."

Terry walked over to Tompkins and bent over with his arms dangling. He patted the dead man's pockets and pulled out a wad of cash and a cell phone, thought they might come in handy. He thought about putting the guy in the trunk, or maybe burying him, before saying, "No one's going to find him today. And Crabtree can't get out of this that easily, right?"

Lancaster tried to smile. "Finding Crabtree is my new reason to live."

Lancaster's arm was in bad shape. Terry lied at the hospital, said it was an accident, that his friend was playing around and set it off.

It was a town surrounded by woods, plenty of hunters here. Mostly, Hattiesburg was home to three campuses worth of college students and plenty of retirees in their walled-and-guarded subdivisions surrounding custom-built lakes.

"You brought the gun?" the doctor asked.

"Jesus, I didn't think about it. After he dropped it, we headed for the car. I can go get it."

"Please—"

"You're not leaving me," Lancaster said, sounding strained as he wrenched his neck to he keep an eye on Terry.

"Fine, I'll stay. I'll run back for it later."

The doctor scanned the papers some ER nurse had shoved in his hand after they started working on Lancaster. "Jesus, that's a lot of lost blood. How far did you drive?"

"We're out in the woods, over in the east." Terry didn't remember much about the area. "Out in Oak Grove?"

"That's west, and not so far."

"I said west, right? It's pretty far."

The doctor shook his head, asked Terry to wait in another room. Lancaster watched him go. No way to avoid the cops in gunshot cases, even accidents. He knew Terry might bolt right now, dye his hair and talk his way onto a bus or taxi and be so gone by the time Lancaster came out of surgery. They'd always told each other that if one gets in trouble, the other saves himself. Theoretically.

The doctor stared Lancaster in the eye. He shouldn't have stared back.

"An accident, huh?"

Lancaster said, "I'm not any good with guns."

"This type of wound, I'm betting someone else wasn't good with it."

"I'm bleeding to death here, and you're calling me a liar?"

The doctor gnawed his lip a moment before shrugging. "Pretty much, yeah. Let's get you prepped."

ELEVEN

Megan Killingsworth carried the plastic grocery bag containing the nurse's uniform to the ladies room at Shoney's a few blocks from the hospital in Hattiesburg. Her boyfriend or pimp or dealer, all three titles losing relevance as the day went on, had bitched her out for buying the thing since it wasn't going to work. She told him she knew, but it was too fucking late. She'd made the charge on the stolen American Express, so there was no way to return it. The boyfriend told her to wash the off the make-up and redo her hair if she was to have a chance at all. That's when she left, walked the five miles from downtown, sweating like shit, to change in this restaurant bathroom.

She hated the costume, thought it was too tight, and it wasn't what she needed anyway. A white nurse's uniform, all they had at the costume shop. She told the lady helping her, "It's not like the ones the nurses on *ER* wear."

The lady sighed. "It's all we've got. We can't just order stuff like we're Sears."

Megan had held the dress to her body, checked the price—not like she cared about price with the card in her pocket. Better than nothing. It wasn't until halfway down Hardy Street she remembered a girl from college she knew bought scrubs at a special store near the hospital.

Stupid, stupid. And I can't use the card again. She'd tried using a Mastercard twice in a day once and barely got out the door of the liquor store. The computers put booby traps on them, no fair at all.

After struggling into the thing, tossing her ripped jeans and pink retro My Little Pony T-shirt into the bag, she tromped out and made her way down the service road to the hospital. She stashed her street clothes deep in a shrub and hoped no one would think to take a look, just call it trash.

Inside, the cold air gave her chills, sweat turning to snow almost. She didn't lose her composure, moved innocently towards the elevator, punched the up button, and waited. She adjusted her hat while wondering where the best place would be to start looking for drugs.

Funny thing was that while she looked really out of place at the hospital, no one stopped her. All the nurses and physicians in their green or white or pink scrubs moved quickly and gave her only passing glances. She felt relieved, then went about her search. Found a stray chart and wandered around looking for open closets, pill bottles, vials, syringes. Some for herself and the rest to sell. She needed rent money to give to the boyfriend—he called himself her "roommate"—who let her pay a little to stay at his place, who sold her dope. She only fucked him when the mood struck her.

Most closets were locked, most rooms empty of good stuff except for a few needles and pain pill sample packs she lifted. The big hauls were guarded by bored and mean nurses. And she counted the pharmacy out without a second thought. Stupid costume, stupid plan, just plain stupid. A friend once rambled around the third floor in *street clothes*, for fuck's sake, and fared better than she was doing. After a while of riding the elevators and trading random charts, searching for an unattended medicine stash, it was quickly obvious that she needed a better plan.

Maybe in the real ER, then. Worth a shot.

She found her way through the halls and got there in time to see a huge commotion, several orderlies and nurses restraining someone howling like a wolf on a gurney. She edged closer, the calmest one of the people-storm surrounding Lancaster. He stopped thrashing for a moment when he noticed her and their eyes met and he said, "Jesus, you're beautiful."

Megan reached for his face, cupped her palm on his cheek. He looked like a guy from a punk band and *Grease* all rolled into one, except for the awful blonde dye job in his hair. "You'll be fine."

"Can you help me?"

"Am I helping now?"

He nodded, teeth chattering.

"I'll be waiting for you when the doctors have finished."

The orderlies pushed her away as they started the bed rolling towards an operating room, and Lancaster was again wailing like it wasn't so much the pain killing him as it was being taken from Megan.

She had to find out more. Lancaster was her ticket out of town.

TWELVE

When Alan walked into the kitchen to find Norm feeding peach slices to Lydia, he wanted to shoot the son of a bitch where he sat. Instead he looked blank, surprised he was already numb to death after only two kills.

Still, it hurt. He was sure Lydia was lying to him now.

She said, "Oh, Alan, you made it. Norm stopped by to pay you the rest of the money."

Norm blinked. "I did?"

Alan leaned against the counter. He took the gun from his pocket, set it beside him, then crossed his arms and bowed his head. He wasn't praying.

Norm forked a peach slice and ate it himself. He reached over with a napkin to wipe the glaze from Lydia's mouth. She shook her head as if to say, *Not with Alan and his gun there.* He said, "I didn't bring any money, Lydia. I can go get some."

"It's fine, tomorrow or the next. However, you do owe Alan now, understand?"

Alan watched as the information sunk in. Norm didn't seem interested in the peaches or Lydia anymore. His hands shook, which almost made Alan laugh, considering how he had been afraid of this asshole at first. Roles reversed, things changed, tides turned.

"I killed your partner," Alan said, blunt as shit, just to watch the guy fall apart even more. Lydia's face wrinkled into anger, a solemn stare aimed Alan's way. He shrugged at her and finally grinned, unable to hold it back anymore.

Lydia turned back to Norm and said, "There's one problem. We'll need to be clear about this, no lies."

"I would never—"

"Shut up and keep listening. Alan's going to help keep you honest, so let's be upfront."

Norm nodded. Alan drifted over until he was standing behind Norm's chair, the redneck unable to see what the big man was doing. Three slices of peaches left. Norm played around with the slices nervously, cutting them into smaller and smaller bits.

"You're not working against us on this, are you? The money, the decision, all your idea, right?" Lydia said.

Norm nodded. "Well, I mean, it was *your* idea."

"No, not at all. Like I said, perfectly clear, you're alone on this?"

"Yes."

"So if I told you Alan was followed by two men today who are now witnesses to this unfortunate loss, you wouldn't know anything about it?"

Norm's fork clattered on the plate. "Jesus."

Alan started to reach for Norm's shoulder. A glance from Lydia stopped him.

"You know these guys?"

"No, I'm telling you, I have no idea. Jesus, there's a witness? We're dead, aren't we? That's why you wanted me saying it was my idea. You're recording all this. A set up!"

Alan said, "Not us, mole man. We're squeaky clean and you're smearing our glass."

"What?"

"Listen to Lydia, all right?"

She sighed heavily and closed her eyes, bobbed her head in a silent count, then said, "Alan didn't have time to kill them. They're not cops. Maybe they were friends of Tompkins. I don't know, but they know who Alan is and they saw what he did. Now, do you know two guys who pick up abandoned cars from the side of the interstate?"

Norm straightened in his chair. "Terry and Lancaster. Man, I didn't know they were still around here. Those two are pretty slick."

"Friends of yours?"

A shrug. "Not really friends. Maybe Randy more than me. They would come looking for a job or trying to unload a decent car. Every once in a while, they'd dip into pills for quick cash. Terry's the smart one, kind of easy-going. The other one's always pissed off."

"Why would they be interested in Tompkins?"

"Maybe they were after Alan."

They went quiet, no one wanting to admit anything.

Norm said, "I can't believe he's dead."

"Want to see his body?" Alan said.

"Are you crazy?"

"Don't wig out on us here. You wanted him dead."

"*You* pushed it on me," Norm said, a finger weakly pointed at Lydia. "I would've just turned on him, called in anonymously. You wanted in on my action."

Lydia said, "And that's not a better deal? Your choice was a thief and liar or someone who actually wants to do things right. So get over it."

Both men shrunk from her, forgetting the chair and the fake arms and legs for a second. Her voice was in command mode. *She* knew the plan, the escape, the details.

She said, "You're in this as we are. If you're really not in with Terry and Lancaster, then you're going to help us find them."

Alan coughed, took in a sharp breath. Lydia kept on.

"They won't say anything to the cops because they'd rather milk Alan for more money. Same with you. *You* won't tell the cops because it turns suspicion on you. Not to mention that you don't want me to look for you, right? That wouldn't be healthy."

Norm sat so still Alan thought he had fainted. He finally shook his head and said, "I understand."

"Get the rest of the money and come back over. We start looking immediately."

"I still owe the rest of the money?"

Lydia glanced at Alan, who smacked Norm in the face. The redneck slid out of the chair, hand to his face, "Shit, shit, shit, shit!"

"Yes, you owe the money, an apology, and you help us find these faggot bastard friends of yours, you got that?"

Norm stayed hunched on the floor. He nodded, wouldn't look at Lydia. "I can't do that."

"Too bad. You have to." Lydia hummed it in a way that had both Alan and Norm melting for her, obvious from their eyes and lips, now paying complete attention. "You both listen to me, and I'm not going to let anything happen to either one of you. Count on it. Now let's start with the money."

Norm found his feet and held his stomach as Alan escorted him to the front door, the redneck growing more feeble with each step.

"If you're going to throw up, save it for outside, will you?" Alan said. "I work hard to keep this place nice for Lydia."

Norm nodded again, no words left after the slap. Alan felt sorry for him in a way, seeing that maybe he didn't expect the killing to work out, like he was just venting steam and Lydia pushed it on him. Pretty much what Alan had tried to do in the first place, just let it go. Too late now. Alan didn't feel so hot after shooting Cap and staging him with Ronnie on the roadside. The thing was, he might have been a little shook up seeing Tompkins beg, but he pulled the trigger and was surprised by a split second of confidence. Thinking the guy deserved to die. Lydia had really done a number on him: *You're one of five billion. You think any God ever imagined that many people? It's the jungle. Be good to those who are good to you, get rid of those who aren't, and the rest can fend for themselves.*

Outside, Alan watched Norm sprint for the truck, gagging the whole way, barely getting the door open before he crouched over and emptied his stomach on the lawn.

Alan let out a sigh, stepped inside and closed the door, feeling a bit of a tug in his own stomach. He cleared his throat. The feeling got worse. By the time he made it to Lydia's bathroom, he didn't have time to lift the toilet lid. He aimed for the shower, all his lunch and acid erupting as he clawed for the cold water tap and let the stream run over the back of his head. It wasn't so much over shooting Tompkins as it was imagining what Lydia had in store by making him work with Norm. The way he was feeding her those peaches, the way she said she wouldn't let anything happen to either one of them. Alan heaved again. He wasn't going to share his Sweetie with anyone.

Lydia heard what Alan told Norm on his way out the door. She heard the sigh, the throat-clearing, and then listened to him being sick, the sounds echoing off the tile and through the house. She stared at the peaches on the table, hoping her tough approach would pay off with Norm so he would return soon. The business wasn't the most important thing. His compliance was. She needed cooperation, because after they found and got rid of the car thieves, the three of them would need to make a quick escape and find a new life elsewhere. A safe place where her two men could worship her in comfort and beauty, where she could mold them from losers into beefcakes.

"Alan, are you okay? Alan?"

She was certain he would get used to the idea of sharing her. *Where else would he ever get a chance to be with someone with even a tenth of what I've got?*

"Alan, sweetie?"

THIRTEEN

Terry paced the hall, thought about leaving, unable to imagine staying free on his own. He was smarter and more slippery than Lancaster but that wasn't always enough. Having a hard-hearted partner covered the other bases. So he stayed, drank bad coffee and read old magazines, ignored the kids playing on the waiting room floor while their greasy parents stared off into space.

A doctor poked his head in about thirty minutes later, motioned for Terry to follow him. Out in the hall, the man mumbled through a few lines. He was thin and tired, with straight white hair topping a young face. He wore a trout pin on his lapel.

"Louder, doc," Terry said.

"This is your brother, right?"

"No, not by blood."

"You're what, then? Life partners, along those lines?"

Terry felt acid rise in his throat. He cleared it. "Excuse me?"

"What I'm saying is he needs blood. We can find some, I'm sure. Family members sometimes are the best bet. Since you're not related, I still want to know if you're compatible. Supplies are pretty low all over."

"We don't match," Terry said. He really had no idea. Terry stifled a belch and swallowed heartburn. Cops would be there soon. Lancaster was an idiot for wanting a real hospital. It was the first time Terry had seen the guy so helpless, although he still radiated vibes that said *Do it or I can still beat you silly with only one good arm.*

The doctor sighed and turned to go, mumbling, "Wait here."

Terry fumed. The doctor thought he was gay. A liar and gay. He called the doctor back. "How long will the surgery be? You're sure he'll be okay?"

"Nothing is sure until we've done it."

"Wild guess, please."

"The arm will never be the same. Maybe seventy percent of normal. This will take hours, so have a seat and we'll keep you updated."

"I could go get the gun, get him a few things, if that'll help."

The doctor shifted his eyes, blinked fast, all the things Terry had learned to control when he wasn't telling the whole truth. "I think it would be better for everyone if you stayed here, maybe called his family, something like that. Just don't leave. In case you do, how can we reach you?"

Terry thought about faking a number before remembering Tompkins' cell phone bulging in his pocket. He pulled it out, opened it, and scrolled the menu. "Hold on a second."

"You don't know your own number?"

"I just got it, you know. Only a couple weeks, and I haven't bothered memorizing. I don't call myself much." Terry found the right screen and read off the number to the doctor, who scribbled it in the margins of his other notes.

As the doctor blended into the other white coats and scrubs down the hall, Terry looked for an elevator. Lancaster would be under for a long time, in no shape to answer questions. Another quick change—hair color, glasses, maybe a scar—and he could come back later. Scrubs might help, and an ID badge. Hard to come by without knocking someone in the head. Lancaster was better at that sort of thing.

The elevator doors opened. Terry stepped inside with a couple of other people and rode to the ground floor. He fought off tears. Shit, he didn't need to be crying. His friend being hurt was one thing. Now they were close to getting caught. Tompkins' body, waiting to be discovered, and the trooper's death still hanging in the air. *Why didn't we take off when we had the chance? Why stick around so fucking long?*

Terry wandered out to the minivan in the emergency room parking lot. Blood slicked the passenger side where Lancaster had leaned against it, soaked the seat where he had writhed, gritting his teeth and begging Terry to drive faster. Terry tapped his fingers on the hood. If the cops ran the plates, they would know it was stolen.

So it all came down to this—just how good a con was he, really? He hoped he and Lancaster had handled the trooper well enough that no one would make the connection. The last resort, even though Terry had wanted to use the information for different ends, was to give the cops Alan Crabtree in exchange for a break.

Terry pounded the hood, hurt his hand. He rubbed the heel of it and decided to go back to inside the hospital. He was hungry, so first a stop at the cafeteria for a sandwich, and then a long wait for consequences.

The uniformed cop stood over Terry in the waiting room, one hand near his gun for no good reason, the other hand fiddling with his radio knob.

"Witnessed a murder?" he said.

Terry nodded. "I think it was a drug thing, out in the woods like that. We surprised him, so he shot before running away."

"What were you doing out in the woods?"

Terry rolled his eyes, played along. "Let's say there are some things my friend and I don't really want others in our life to know about, see?"

The cop took a step back, almost unconsciously, exactly what Terry hoped for. This was one of those tough guy cops with beefy arms but flabby middles because lifting dumbbells was easier than doing the whole routine. Hair was close, no sideburns. His shirt was tight, the open collar showing a bright white T-shirt underneath. Terry thought it must be brand new. The cop's partner was talking to the doctor, probably hearing an exaggerated story based on thin suspicions. Not long before they would start to play hardball with him.

"You want to describe this guy, then?"

"Maybe. I can try, but he was a fat one. Fat guys all look alike to me."

"What?"

Terry stood, stretched out his arms and faked a yawn, then propped a hand on his hip. "I saw this big guy with a gun. The face is a blur. Red-haired? Light brown? I can't remember."

Stall. Keep the info close to the vest. Keep the story confused until you see a way out. All this strategy floated through Terry's head while he acted like a swish to keep the goddamn cop at arm's length. That's all it was, an innocent romp in the woods.

"Anything else? Clothing? His car?"

"Nothing comes to mind, officer." *He knows you're a cop killer. Get out of here. Run, hurry.*

Terry kept his eyes sleepy-lidded and his shoulders slumped. The officer's partner appeared in the doorway, flicked his fingers in a silent *Come here.* The flabby cop stepped over and they whispered at each other before the partner, a younger and more chiseled type, spoke police codes into his shoulder mike. Terry knew most of those, listened hard.

The cop kept his voice down. Nothing but bits and pieces. Probably sending cops to check out the murder story.

The older cop fumbled a path back to Terry, who sat with his arms crossed. The younger cop followed, fingers outstretched and twitching.

"Stay here. We'll need to talk to you further."

Terry nodded. The sleepiness wasn't much of an act, and he needed the rest. Hey, if the cops found the body, maybe they would believe him. If not, they'd probably start trying to untangle his story. It didn't matter then if he was telling the truth or spinning more lies. If it got that far, bye-bye Alan Crabtree.

From the doorway, a sad nurse stopped and watched him. He watched back, wishing she would go away. Like a statue, a petite girl with thin streaked hair, barrettes holding it up, eye-makeup like the alternachicks on MTV. She was cute, her uniform a white dress, white stockings, white cap. Terry didn't think nurses dressed like that anymore.

The nurse walked into the room and stood over him. He was too tired to say something smart-ass or threatening. She patted his arm.

"Your friend. I hope he's okay." That's all she said before walking out.

Terry drifted to sleep imagining he was in the audience at the talk show on TV, watching Crabtree and Lancaster confront each other about their "feelings" while holding long thin knives.

FOURTEEN

No amount of tough backwoods attitude was enough to prepare Norm for Tompkins' stiff bloody corpse. The ants were swarming. Eyes and mouth open wide, still shocked. Alan had followed the redneck into the woods and knew they were in the right spot when Norm spun with a yelp and slammed into Alan like he wasn't there before hiding behind his bulk.

"I guess Terry didn't clean up like I told him to." Alan said, fighting to act like he was comfortable around a dead body.

"You did that? You shot Randy and left him here?"

"I didn't *mean* to leave him here. I was interrupted. Help me out."

Alan shook out the curtains he had picked up from his house. They were dark dusty things he shoved in the closet after putting up olive green blinds. Norm took one side and helped straighten them on the ground beside Tompkins. He wouldn't look in his former partner's direction, making the whole damn operation awkward. The skin was already drained of color except the purple settling on the backs of Tompkins' arms and legs.

"You're going to have to touch him so we can get him on the curtain," Alan said.

Norm's mouth went wide, his eyes crunched tight. "You didn't say anything about that before."

"It was fucking *assumed*, wasn't it? Jesus, you're too much, man."

It was Lydia's idea that Alan and Norm go back to the woods, laughing at Terry's tit for tat plea. Alan thought taking along the curtains was probably a good precaution. Terry and Lancaster might not go running to the cops on a normal occasion, but with one of them shot, who knew?

"Grab the legs. At least he's got sandals you can hold onto."

Alan grabbed Tompkins' wrists and lifted, barely getting help from

Norm, who touched the body as if it were a bucket of plague. They scooted Tompkins' ass over the curtain and dropped the body dead center. Tompkins landed on his side, arms and legs splayed in crazy angles.

"Did you bring the shovel?" Alan said.

Norm shook his head. "I'll get it. Give me the keys."

"It's unlocked. I promise."

When Norm got back with the shovel, Alan dug up the dirt he thought might have soaked in blood, tossed it in with Tompkins. It was impossible to get all of the forensic evidence out of the way. Not like it mattered in Stone County, Mississippi. The cops sure as hell weren't going to analyze the type of groove the shovel made in the dirt.

Nearby, Alan found Lancaster's gun, wondered why he forgot to take it along before. He picked it up and tossed it on Tompkins.

"We carry him back to the car?" Norm asked in a pissy voice.

Alan breathed in his direction for a long moment, eyes closed.

"Okay, fine, gee…" Norm lifted Tompkins' feet.

He kept dropping his end, so Alan said, "Move," and dragged the dead guy by the neck back to the Kia. They folded him into the trunk and left. Alan turned north.

"You think they would try to hole up and take care of Lancaster's arm? Something like that? Maybe find a doctor's house, like in *The Getaway*."

"Those two? I thought you knew them."

"Not very well, but I'm just saying what I would do, I guess."

"I'm guessing that the way they dress and talk and gel up their hair, they headed straight for the hospital."

"What about Randy?"

Alan looked over his shoulder, like he really had to check. "No time. He can come, too."

The closest hospital was in Hattiesburg. They made it around four in the afternoon. Alan and Norm found the minivan in the front lot easily, then circled wide looking for surveillance. Nothing obvious. They decided to play safe—park in a far corner, stand outside the car, and wait for something to happen.

"How the hell can we kill them in the hospital? Why do we need to kill them at all?" Norm said while he paced around Alan, who was calm as the sky.

"I'm willing to negotiate."

"Yeah, but still—"

"Here's a question," Alan said. "You say you know these guys, or Tompkins did, or whatever. What are their real names?"

Norm thought about it, wrinkled his brow and hummed a low note. "I have no idea. We're sure those are fake names, absolutely. I've never thought too hard about it."

"I wonder what that would be worth to them, someone finding out who they really are?"

"Don't know how you'd figure it."

Alan crossed his arms, grinned. "Just thinking out loud."

Norm looked at his watch. "What next?"

"I think you should go see your good buddy Lancaster and then come tell me what's going on."

"You're not coming?"

"I don't think you've shot anyone who's currently a patient in that hospital. Maybe Terry won't tell them everything, but he's dumb enough to say it was a fat guy who did it."

Norm guessed that even with fake names and a cover story, Terry and Lancaster would stick out, be easy to find. He was right. After a quick start in ER, asking the calm and patient types who had probably been sitting there an hour and would sit a lot longer unless they started yelling and screaming, he shrugged around to anyone in scrubs with this sad look, describing his "friend" Lancaster. Finally, he got some help from a younger black woman with very short hair, coal dark except for light brown streaks, and a smile like the welcoming face of God, Norm thought. She led him through corridors and asked other nurses, doctors, and finally a security guard. Norm wasn't crazy about asking him. Good thing he didn't have any idea and didn't seem to care.

Finally she came back from a huddle with several other women in green scrubs and told him, "He's in recovery. The surgery went better than they hoped."

"That's great. Wow."

"Isn't it?" The nurse reached out for a hug, and Norm gave her a big one. She smelled like apples and cinnamon, and Norm nearly forgot he was only pretending to be happy for Lancaster.

"You can't see him now," the nurse said.

"When could I?"

"It'll be a few hours. I could show you the waiting room."

"That'll be fine."

She led him to the elevator. Once inside, she took his hand. He wondered if she was this way with all strangers or if she was reacting to his charm. Maybe she liked him. He grinned, thought about how that could go down right there in the elevator.

The nurse said, "I see too much trouble in this place, more heartbreak than healing sometimes. So when I hear about this friend of yours being all right, I think, *Praise Jesus*, you know?"

"Sure."

"That's it. Glory."

It didn't stop his fantasy to hear her talk gospel. Figured it might be sexy for her to shout "Thank you Jesus" while they pounded away.

He was really thinking about Lydia, how sweet she was earlier, inviting him over and treating him like a friend. Until Alan got home, at least. Then she did the cold bitch routine. He understood, though. Part of the new business arrangement. She told him it was necessary in order to keep Alan in line. *He can be a wild man. Sometimes, I don't know why I let him drag me into this...*

Lydia was so grateful to Norm for opening the can of peaches and feeding them to her. She'd been dying for peaches, she said. He forked them, held them close to her lips, and she playfully chattered her teeth for each one, laughing like a grown woman instead of the feisty sixteen year old he remembered ripping his clothes off in the band closet.

Could he really see himself at her side for longer than a curious fuck? A fifty/fifty partner? The fakes arms and legs were good, but they had to come off sometime, and then what would he think? She was a freak who manipulated the hell out of any man she wanted. He was seeing her a little more clearly—the woman twisting his balls, that's what it was. She didn't want *part* of the business, only the whole shebang.

"Sir? This is the floor."

The bell dinged and the doors started to slide shut. He was so spaced when they opened, he was still seeing pictures in his daydreams.

Norm leapt for the doors, wedged through, and tried to remember what he was doing here. The nurse had gone back with the elevator. He was on his own.

The waiting room. Supposed to find the waiting room. No, Recovery. Where was Recovery? He spun slowly, looking for a sign on the wall.

The air was warmer, more uncomfortable than on the other floors. Not as many people around except a faded-out middle-aged woman sitting in a chair by the window, staring at him. Behind her, the city was gray, the window tinting wavy and full of bubbles.

"Where's Recovery?" Norm said to the woman.

"Second floor."

"They sent me up here."

She shrugged, rubbed her lips with a pinkie finger. "Really, it's down there far as I know."

Norm took a walk down the hall, glancing at room numbers and hoping the woman was wrong. Empty carts lined the wall, almost like the floor was being used as a storage closet. Around the corner, a TV made indistinguishable noise, commercial jingles obscuring the voices. He peeked into the room. Bright lights and plush chairs filled too much space. Scattered kids' toys on the floor, and the TV on a cart in the corner. One guy sat slumped in a chair in front of it. He turned his head as Norm walked in.

It was Terry. He wrinkled his face a moment before his eyes shot wide. "You!"

Norm was frozen in the doorway.

"Your partner said you were trying to get him killed. Looks like you did it."

Norm couldn't say a damn word. Not one goddamn word.

Terry pushed himself out of the chair. He was rough, his clothes stained with dried blood and dirt, his hair stuck in a slope. "How the hell did you know where to find me? You going to kill me too? Right here in the hospital?"

Norm held his hands out, low but spread wide, wanting to say *Back off, man*, not able to make his mouth work. So he turned and ran, slipping on the tiles, scuttling enough to catch hold and make it back to the elevators. He slammed the Down button—onetwothreefourFIVE—the lights above showed it on the second floor. Blinked off, then on again at the first.

Stairs. Norm needed the stairs and almost ran the way he had just ran from. Terry was coming now, walking fast, face flushed. Norm took off, ignoring the woman telling him to slow down. A few people in scrubs ducked their heads out of rooms to see what the commotion was. A pretty nurse in a white dress watched Norm and Terry calmly like the chase was on TV.

An "Exit" sign ahead. No, a "Fire Exit". Fuck it, let it go. Norm glanced over his shoulder. Terry was still coming, fast-walking, intense as hell. The door ahead warned Norm in bold letters not to take these stairs except in emergencies. He thought, *Close enough*, then pushed his way through.

The alarm blared sudden and digital, lights flashing in the stairwell as he took them down by twos and kept tripping. People started filing out at the halfway point, blocking the steps, turning it into an orderly evacuation. Norm nudged past and kept looking back, not seeing Terry in the sea of faces but knowing he was there somewhere.

FIFTEEN

When the alarms went off, Terry took the stairs to the second floor and bounded over to the recovery room door like he didn't have a clue. A cop tried to hold him back.

"What's with the alarms?" Terry said.

"Someone triggered a fire alarm. Probably false," the cop said, easing off a bit.

"My friend's okay?"

A smirk from the cop. "Fine, yeah."

Terry backed off, the cop's pistol in his hand. "Take me in there."

The cop reached for his gun, the empty holster confusing him until he figured it out. "Jesus."

"I want to go in. Hit the button."

The cop reached for the big round button that opened the doors to recovery. They swung wide and Terry directed the cop to go ahead of him.

"Calm down, buddy. This isn't going to help your friend," the cop said. His eyes flicked left and right.

"It helps *me* if you do what I tell you. Get in there." Terry waved the gun and gave the cop a shove. He followed close behind and slammed the round button on the inside wall. The doors closed. Two rows of beds, some with curtains between them, very few with patients, crowded the walls. A couple of nurses, one frazzled and brunette, maybe fifty, and the other a young plump redhead, both saw the gun and wheezed together like asthma was contagious.

Lancaster was near the back, the most pale and vulnerable Terry had ever seen him. Asleep, IV tube snaking up his good arm, a yellow-stained cast on the other.

Terry pointed with the gun. "Is he out cold? Can I wake him up?"

The cop looked at the nurses. One nodded, the other shook her head. The cop said, "Hell if I know."

Terry forced the cop and nurses against the opposite wall while he held the gun at them and backpedaled to Lancaster, shook his shoulder. No response. He did it again, a little harder, and his friend stirred.

"Stop it," Lancaster said.

"You feel any pain?"

"I can't feel my tongue."

"We need to get the hell out of here, man. Right now. You and your fucking hospital. Jackass."

Lancaster's eyes blinked fast and then were wide open. He lifted his good arm a little, groaned, then tried his legs. "Shit that hurts."

"Well?"

Lancaster cringed a little. "I can do it. Get this IV out of me."

Terry pulled the needle out with one hand while still holding the gun steady on the cop and nurses. The alarm seemed far away now that they were numb to it. Scuffling in the hallway was muffled, but the recovery room felt quiet except for rustling sheets, amplified. Lancaster swung his legs over and took deep breaths. Terry hooked his friend's good arm and helped him stand. Little grunts and teeth gritting, Lancaster taking it well. When it was over, he nodded at Terry.

"Thanks. Where's that girl?"

"What girl? Your gown's falling off."

"Where are my clothes?"

"No fucking clue, man. Let me tie this up." Terry handed the gun to Lancaster, the automatic heavy in his hand. Terry tugged the gown into place and tied the strings. The cop started forward, a tiny step, hands out to his side.

Lancaster's arm moved on reflex, stiff as iron and the gun steady. "Don't underestimate me, man."

"Be cool."

"I'm doped up. I'm cool as shit. Just stay back where you were, back there, get back back baaaaack."

Terry said, "What have they got you on?"

"Ambrosia, man. Nectar."

The gown was on tight as gowns could be. Terry took the gun back and led Lancaster like he was an old lady. Half way to the door, Lancaster had his bearings. The nurses watched with shocked grins.

The cop said, "You think you're getting out of here?"

Terry slammed the big round button and followed Lancaster out the door shouting, "Think it? I never doubted it."

Alan guessed that the flood of people spilling from the hospital exits wasn't a good sign. He dropped into the driver's seat of the Kia and started the engine. He had only driven ten feet when Norm appeared out of nowhere in front of him. Alan braked hard and Norm pounded the hood. His hair was wild and he was out of breath. Alan unlocked the door. Norm opened it and sat down without a word about Alan almost leaving him. Alan wondered when the thought might pop into Norm's head. They kept moving out of the parking lot slowly while Alan looked into the crowds for Terry and Lancaster.

"This your fault?" Alan said.

"They're here. You were right. Shit, Terry got after me."

Alan turned to him. "Got after you? Like chased?"

Norm shrugged, bobbed his head, front window, back window. "He was pissed, I tell you. Lancaster's in recovery. You messed his arm up good."

Alan wanted to punch the guy. All he was supposed to do was find out if they were here and where. That's all. Another glance into the swelling crowd, patients in wheelchairs and robes, young interns in scrubs, doctors, a tiny nurse in a white dress, the kind he had seen in old movies. She looked out of place. Alan remembered what Terry had been wearing in the woods. Trying to find that shirt, or the ball cap—the right ball cap. Get them in the car and put an end to this.

A glimpse, guy helping another guy on the sidewalk. One in a hospital gown. Alan craned his neck as the car passed. Right there, it had to be them.

"Jesus, Alan!"

He snapped back to the road in front of him, neon green and silver filling the windshield. A fire-truck coming straight at the car fast. Where were the sirens? The flashing lights? They were too close. Alan braked hard, bouncing Norm's forehead off the dash. The truck kept coming, kept coming, didn't stop.

It crunched the front of the Kia like tin foil, a loud pop followed by the windshield exploding and the car sliding backwards while Alan twisted the steering wheel.

Then, crazy noise in Alan's ears—sirens and yelling and fuck all people outside tapping on the driver's window asking if he was all right. Norm was holding his face, yelling his throat raw. Alan turned but faces were in his way, the whole car surrounded by firemen and doctors, no sign of Terry and Lancaster. Alan beat the steering wheel with his palm and began to cry. Heaving crying, vacuum breaths, nothing left inside but sheer fucking hate.

SIXTEEN

"I'm in a hospital gown, barely able to walk, and nobody in that crowd noticed?" Lancaster said as Terry helped him into the minivan.

"The alarm distracted them, and then the fire truck hit a car."

Lancaster slowly pulled his knees up and inside. Terry eased the seat into a deep recline. Lancaster sucked air as he leaned back.

"Where to?" Terry said.

"We need a few days. I need some clothes, lot of dope, cable TV. We got enough for a casino hotel or something?"

"The hospital was bad enough. I'm thinking we go someplace with not so many security cameras. Then we should bolt. Ever been to Michigan?"

Lancaster winced. "Jesus, that's cold."

"It's beautiful."

"Cold."

"We'll talk it out on the way to the Coast. Grab something at Holiday Inn, Motel 6, one of those."

"What about that girl, man? The nurse?"

"You're hallucinating."

"No, she touched me. Before I was doped."

Terry closed the door gently, wondered if the poor guy meant that little nurse in the white dress. Things turning all *Twilight Zone*. Lancaster was on the verge of sleep anyway. *No more hedging*, Terry thought. They really needed to get out of town, out of state. A little hip college town somewhere, maybe get real jobs until the cash flow was established enough for them to start small with con games, then return to the car business. Terry smiled and flipped the keys around the ring as he walked behind the van and started towards the driver's door. One more glance towards the commotion, and he noticed a big wall of man stomping towards him. Alan Crabtree, blood on his face and hands, concentrated single-minded on Terry, fast steps.

Terry fumbled the keys and leapt for the door. He got inside and hit the lock button, turned the ignition and pumped the gas just as Crabtree's face and hands thumped into the window and smudged blood and spit. He pounded a palm on the window. Terry couldn't take his eyes off him, froze in mid-shift. The man had red eyes, puffy cheeks. Crying? What the hell?

A couple of firemen and an intern followed, grabbing Crabtree's shoulders and easing him off the van. A fireman mouthed *I'm sorry* to Terry, who waved and nodded. The men patted Crabtree's back as he seemed to lose even more composure. They walked him towards the hospital without giving the van another look.

Terry sat for another minute, the engine idling, hand on the gearshift. Lancaster was asleep and hadn't stirred at all when Crabtree slobbered on the window. The smears were drying, clouding up the view. Terry shifted into drive and made his way out of the parking lot.

When Alan was away for too long, Lydia called her neighbor for help with little things. This time she needed water because her throat was dry. The neighbor was glad to help, but she stayed too long chattering away about her family and her job at a casino hotel. Here was a woman in her mid-thirties, same as Lydia, who looked so much older, her hair already with wisps of gray surrounding a hard face. She wore faded jeans, tight sandals, and a Bugs Bunny T-shirt. So far out of Lydia's league, a wasted life of ordinary. After all Lydia went through, she swore to never settle for less than she thought she deserved.

Lydia hoped Alan would call soon. She was getting worried—both for her guys and the possibility they might lead the police to her. *She* was the mastermind. The dirty work boys always got reduced sentences.

As the neighbor babbled about her son's problems with his girlfriend, Lydia thought, *Fuck the police. What worse punishment can they give me than this?* They kill her, all the trouble would go away. They stick her in jail, the scenery might be lacking. She would miss her curtains, miss the sex, miss the thrill she got when these men followed her orders and pampered her.

"I think she's cheating on him," the neighbor said.

It jerked Lydia back to the real world. "What?"

"My son's girlfriend is probably cheating. You can just tell. At that age, you'd think his world is ending."

"Women hold all the power. It's like a fuse blows in them when we hold out."

The neighbor stared and crossed her arms. "Are you all right?"

"You want to do your son some good? Teach him right up front that *we* will decide the rest of his life for him, and the best he can do is beat out the other males for the prize."

The neighbor glanced at the curtains, always billowing, and the front door. "I've got to go. Please, if you need anything, call me. Not this afternoon, though, I can't."

The phone rang. Lydia said, "I'll see you later. I've been expecting this one."

When the woman opened the front door, Lydia spoke into her headset mike and waited for the click.

"Hello?"

"Yeah, it's me," Norm said.

"Are you okay? Is Alan all right?"

"We bruised pretty badly. A fire-truck hit us. I'll explain later."

"Can Alan talk?"

"They've got him restrained right now." Norm lowered his voice. "He's crazy, I'm telling you. Crying and thrashing and shit."

Lydia closed her eyes. "Tell me everything."

As Norm spoke, Lydia imagined life in a jail cell, bright walls and a small window too high for her to see through. No motorized wheelchair, only a regular one, a guard constantly watching. No one to do whatever she asked, even if she said "Please." And plenty of people to do whatever they wanted to her.

"There's one thing, and I don't know what's going to happen," Norm said.

"And what is that?"

"We didn't get our, um, *package* out of the trunk yet."

The doctors told Norm to hold ice on his nose. The Kia was totaled. Someone called the rental company and the tow truck. After calling Lydia, Norm walked back to Alan's bedside and listened to the big man's breaths. They sounded like growling. A nurse in an old-fashioned white dress came near the foot of the bed and stared sadly for a moment. She hugged herself and wandered away.

Norm leaned over and whispered, "We should leave very quickly."

Alan yanked at the leather restraints on his wrists. "Can you get these off before anyone notices?"

"Not yet."

"Then shut up."

Norm flinched. "You know, the stuff in our trunk—"

Another yank. "It's too late now. And you know what? The goddamn car is rented in Lydia's husband's name. So everybody's ass is hanging out in the wind now."

The big man relaxed onto the bed. The doctors had split his sleeves from cuff to shoulder, which reminded Norm of the old Incredible Hulk show. Norm's injuries were worse, but Alan looked more beat up—cuts on his face from the glass and bruises from the steering wheel leaving marks that would be there for a while. It made hiding hard to do.

"They should be towing the car soon," Norm said. "Is there anything in it we need?"

Alan shook his head. "Other than the body and my gun, no." He laughed. "Small things."

Norm clapped his hands one time and held up a finger. Even patients looked. He waited until everyone went back to what they were doing before he mumbled to Alan, "I got the gun."

"You kidding?"

"You dropped it, I picked it up."

"How'd you get it in here? Aren't there metal detectors and shit?"

Norm shrugged. "They got us inside so quickly, rushing and shit, I don't think they noticed if there was an alarm or not, especially when the fire alarm stuff happened."

"That was your fault. Just wait. One look at the tapes from the hall cameras, man—"

"So let's bolt."

"And then what? You know how to steal a car?" Alan turned his head away from Norm. "I'm giving up. I was fooling myself anyway."

Norm circled the bed and crouched so he could make eye contact with Alan. "Look at me. Lydia told me to tell you she wants us home now. I don't care how we get there. We need to help her out, you know, especially if they trace the car."

Alan's face was stone.

"You love her, man. You haven't screwed that up yet, so let's get out of here," Norm said. He had unfastened Alan's wrist while talking, almost a sleight of hand thing. "Leave it there a second."

He crept back around the bed and unfastened the other restraints on the ankles and left wrist. Then he stuck his head around the divider, looked both ways, then said, "We should walk straight out, fast as we can. Anyone says anything, we walk faster. They try to stop us, we fight them off. As for a ride, why not take an ambulance?"

Alan thought it was silly, impossible, and their only option. He sat up. "Let's go."

SEVENTEEN

Only Megan took notice of the two men, one huge and one skinny, her arms wrapped around a chart as she watched until they slipped through the doors into the waiting room. She had given up the dope search the moment she saw Lancaster. If these two guys were going after him, then she needed to follow. She ran to the doors as they swung shut. The two men fast-stepped it to the main doors and were gone.

She quick-stepped through the waiting room, the sliding glass doors. The two men were climbing into an ambulance outside the ER. Then she saw the larger of the two patients pull a guy from the passenger seat and drop him on the ground. He was moving, definitely not dead. Not very conscious either.

As the men climbed into the cab the brake lights flashed and the smaller man gunned the engine. The doors closed. Before the ambulance started forward, the nurse sprinted and hopped onto the back bumper. She tried the door. It opened, and she fought the motion and gravity of the van turning right into traffic enough to swing inside and fall over an empty stretcher. The fat man turned and stared.

"Give me the gun," he told the driver.

"I can't let you do that—"

The fat man reached for the driver's back, came out holding a pistol that had been shoved in his waistband. He held it steady on the nurse.

"Get out," he said.

She pushed herself into a crouch, knees to her chin and hands over her head. "I want to go with you."

"No. Jump out. We'll stop."

The driver said, "We can't stop, Alan. Jesus, come on, she's fine for now."

The fat man, Alan, loosened his grip on the pistol. She took a closer look at him. The face was scratched, but it was like a mask. The lines around his eyes were melancholy, not the look of a hardcore killer. A kindred soul, she thought.

"Alan?" she said.

He nodded, waved the gun at her like a finger. "You?"

"Megan."

"Why'd you jump in with us?"

She shrugged. "You're after those other two guys? The one that was shot?"

Norm whistled low. "We've got us a spy. She knows too much."

"Shut up, asshole." Alan rapped the guy's knuckle with the gun. The ambulance swerved when Norm jerked his hand off the wheel and shook it.

Alan said, "You saw the two guys?"

"The cops were here earlier asking questions. They didn't really believe his story, like an accidental shooting while they were in the woods. Some gay thing."

"So what did the cops do?"

"Not much. They were going to check out the story, go to the woods. Then a little while ago the fire alarm went off, so we had to get out of there for a while. I saw those guys heading for a van, then the truck hit your car, and you went after that van before anyone could stop you."

She spoke low and calm, kept her hands still. The big man took in her body, her face, but didn't seem turned on. Megan wondered about that.

He said, "Why so interested in us?"

She hummed in her throat before answering carefully, "Something about the guy who was shot. I want to see him again."

Alan was quiet for so long after that. What was he thinking? Her story sounded crazy even to her, so what would the sad man with the gun and this skittish driver think of it? Not long after, Alan nodded at her, no expression on his face, and turned around in his seat.

"Norm, the siren, man. Turn on the siren."

Lydia wasn't happy to see them after all.

"A stolen ambulance and some little whore nurse?"

"She's a hostage. We didn't have a choice," Norm said.

"Didn't you have a gun?" Lydia examined Megan while speaking, an unblinking burn at this flat-chested kid, barrettes in her hair, who never flashed one emotion the entire five minutes she'd been standing there.

Quiet, too.

Alan stepped over to Lydia's side and ran his fingers through her hair. She didn't smile, but it calmed her. She was glad to be touched.

He said, "We can't have a killing spree. We're in enough trouble already. She can stick around until time for us to leave, which is very soon."

Lydia couldn't keep the whine out of her words. "I can't blame you for the truck hitting you, but did you have to leave that stuff in the trunk? Why didn't you take care of that first?"

"Time and effort. We prioritized. If Norm hadn't set off the alarm, I'll bet this would be a different conversation. So, the car traces back to you. The cops are looking for an ambulance, the one parked down the street. How about we get in my car and go, right?"

Megan strolled easily around the den, touching the paintings, the curtains, the furniture. Lydia could tell this girl was a sponge, acting indifferent and distant, probably soaking in every word they spoke, every detail of the room, so much evidence to use against them later. Lydia wanted her gone, out of the way for good. A *message* to her boys about whom deserved the most attention. Alan seemed okay, still stroking her hair. Norm tripped back and forth—trying so hard to keep his peep show on Megan private, but he wasn't fast or smart enough. When the time was right, Lydia knew all she had to do was nod at Alan, and the girl would die.

"If we take the car, how can you bring my chair?"

Alan said, "We can't. We bring the manual chair, and I take care of you. That's the only way right now.

A flash of her prison nightmare. A flash of helplessness. A flash of her husband fucking the floozy, Norm fucking Megan, and all Lydia could do was watch, wishing her phantom limbs could do more than itch. Touch her own breasts, touch herself down there. Slap the shit out of Norm, too. Claw the little nurse.

"I need my chair, sweetie," she said.

He knelt beside her. "No. There's no room to debate this. I say we've got less than ten minutes."

Lydia wasted another minute quietly trying to think of a better way. She finally spoke trembling commands into her headset mike. She said to Alan, "The safes. We'll need the money. My old chair is in the guest room."

Alan stood and walked off towards the guest room. Norm plopped onto the couch and crossed his feet on the coffee table. Megan had circled the room and now circled Lydia's chair. Her nurse's uniform was so old fashioned, Lydia wondered if Megan was even a nurse at all. Another con, like everyone else in the house. Rented a nice costume and faked her way into a hospital coincidentally on the day Lancaster showed up with a bullet in him.

"You've kept your legs in such nice shape for a quad," the girl said.

"Thank you. How sweet."

"They're fake legs," Norm said. "She lost all her limbs and had these made."

Megan took a step back, almost with a grin on her face. "Really?"

"Norm, that's enough," Lydia said. To the nurse, she said, "Yes, arms and legs are all prosthetic."

"If he hadn't said that—"

"Please, I understand. I don't like to talk about it."

Norm said, "I can tell her if you don't feel like it."

Another of Lydia's daydream images blasted away. Not the clean-cut man in a suit, contacts instead of his thick glasses. He really didn't get it.

"Norm, please get a bottle of strawberry water out of the refrigerator for me, okay?"

He sprang from the couch, smiled wide and thought he was doing her a favor. She really wanted him out of sight for as long as possible. There wasn't any strawberry water in the kitchen at all. She knew he would keep looking and looking until he was absolutely sure.

The nurse kept standing there, barely moving a muscle except her head—the tiniest nod Lydia had ever seen, aimed right for her, a message from God.

She would have sent her own message—*Drop dead bitch*—if she wasn't so afraid.

EIGHTEEN

Terry was watching a dating show set on a cruise ship when Lancaster woke up. They were in a decent enough chain hotel on the beach in Gulfport, twin beds and cable TV. Half a Subway sandwich was wrapped up on the table. Terry wolfed down the other half and hoped Lancaster would be strong enough to eat.

Lancaster said, "I want to shave my head."

"What?"

"My head, my hair. When I'm dreaming, I see myself with dark hair. Then I remember it's all dyed right now. I don't like it."

"It'll grow out."

"Yeah, that takes months. I want to shave it and start over now."

His voice was stronger than Terry expected for a guy still recovering from surgery. Lancaster slept during the ride, stirred enough for Terry to help him into the room, then passed out again. Terry went to a Rite Aid for lots of painkillers, probably not strong enough to really help, and some beer. They sold cheap beach clothes, so he bought a few pair of swim trunks and T-shirts. Then he grabbed the sandwich and came back to the room. Two hours of TV—*Dr. Phil* and local news and *Shipmates*.

"It's not a bad idea. They'll be on the lookout for us again, anyway. You shave your head, I try brown dye, maybe a touch of red," Terry said.

"Faggot."

Terry roughed his fingers through his spiky-do and pretended to get interested in the TV show. He hoped Lancaster was just kidding. He didn't feel anything sexual for the guy, not at all. Still, he hadn't fucked a girl in a year and spent most of his time with Lancaster. Then he stayed to help the guy instead of following their emergency plan—run.

Neither spoke for a while. The couple on *Shipmates* hated each other and traded nasty little barbs over a candlelit dinner. Finally, the guy tossed his water on the bitch after all this "You're not as much man as you think you are" shit she was saying. Terry laughed.

Lancaster said, "I'm sorry."

"What've you got to be sorry for?"

"The name calling, a joke."

A shrug. "Didn't bother me. Wasn't funny, though. No one ever said you were a laugh riot."

Another stretch of silence lasted through two commercials.

Lancaster propped himself on his good elbow. "Why didn't you take off, anyway. We always said if one got caught, the other bolts. Right?"

Terry kept his eyes on the screen. "Nothing came to mind, you know. What, get the cars on my own? Run games without backup?"

"Anything's better than getting caught. Still, you've got balls of steel. Holding the gun on that cop? I'm proud of you."

"My story wasn't going over and once they went out to the woods, that would've been it. Finished. So I stuck around. I didn't want you in some drug haze rolling over on me anyway."

Lancaster barked. Pretty damn close to a bark, anyway. "I don't even know your real name! You don't know mine. That's how we arranged this whole thing, remember? Impossible to give each other up."

Terry turned his head. Lancaster was on fire, breathing too hard. If it hurt, he hid it well. "You said it, not me. Can't give each other up. Want some Aleve?"

After shaking his head, Lancaster eased himself down. Then he said, "All right, give me one."

Terry shook one of the painkillers from its bottle and stepped over to the sink, got a cup of water. He took both to Lancaster, placed the pill on his tongue, then slid his hand behind his friend's neck. He lifted Lancaster's head and tilted the glass just so. Lancaster swallowed most of it.

Terry placed the cup on the nightstand and sat on the other bed.

"I'm not mad or anything. You took some risks, and that's okay," Lancaster said.

Terry figured that was the closest thing to a Thank You he was going to get. If the roles were reversed, Lancaster would've been long gone, leaving Terry to his fate. It depressed Terry to realize it, letting it take hold in his brain. Without Lancaster, he was a half-decent slick talker with some good ideas. Meet up with the wrong crowd or a bad sucker, lights out Mr. Terry. He needed the brawn more than Lancaster needed him. On his own, Lancaster was a lone wolf, taking what he needed, no questions asked, no consequences. A rock hard killer.

Terry stared at his sleeping partner for a long time, resenting his dependence on Lancaster, yet so glad to have him safe and sound.

He slipped into sleep and dreamed about Crabtree, who was always small in his dreams. Not thin small but overall, like half-scale. The guy was a clown, a little whimpering mite. This time the half-scale Crabtree was shooting Lancaster again and again and there was so much fucking blood. Lancaster was a video game character, fractured pixels pouring more blood than he could possibly have in his system. Terry watched it happen and hated it, unable to make himself stop it, the way dreams sometimes freeze us into their programs.

Crabtree went from blubber to Lee Marvin in a matter of weeks. It didn't make much sense. They knew the guy was an odd job man, nickel and dime stuff, but a killer tied in with an ecstasy dealer? The rumors were saying something about him being a top-notch hit man. Terry had been out of the loop and thought it was a lark. Now he wanted to ask around and find out. Otherwise, this fat little bastard was going to waste both of them.

In the dream, Crabtree reduced Lancaster to a bloody pile. Then he turned to Terry, still frozen. The fear wasn't in getting shot; it was in Crabtree being the one doing it. But he didn't shoot. He floated. Closer and closer, that bubble of a face on fire like it was when he slammed into the van window. Closer.

Something touched his shoulder.

Terry shouted, swung the sheets wide and sat up in bed. The room was dark except for late afternoon sunlight streaming through a slit in the curtain, enough for Terry to see a Lancaster-shaped blob standing by the bed, bare-chested and mostly bald. Little patches of hair he missed looked like weeds on concrete. His eyes were too bright.

"Calm down. But wake up," he said.

Terry rubbed his face and yawned. "What are you doing? You shouldn't be standing up."

"Had to piss, then got tired of seeing the blonde in my hair. I told you once."

Lancaster didn't look tired or injured except for the cast holding his arm together. He scared Terry a little, the head-shaving being so impulsive like maybe getting shot changed the way Lancaster looked at things, no more sitting back and waiting.

"What do you want?" Terry said.

"I was just thinking about what you said, Crabtree coming to look for us and how weird that was. He's scared we'll tell the cops?"

"He probably thinks we'll blackmail him. I guess I figured we would, too."

"Then he won't stop looking. What if we got in touch, met somewhere in public, and told him we'd let it all go away for a flat fee? Or that we'll lock it away and he can owe us a favor."

Terry thought this was too much thinking from Lancaster. Guess he had to do *something* while shaving his head.

"I don't get it," Terry said. "Out of sight, out of mind, right?"

"I want to get out of here, too. Florida, man. Fuck Michigan or wherever it is you said. We go down to Tampa and set up shop. First priority, though, is settling this with Crabtree."

"Settle what?" Before those two words left his mouth, he already knew the answer.

Lancaster mumbled. "I run away from this, word'll get around. What good will I be? If I fuck up Crabtree real good, word'll be in my favor. Simple payback, that's all I'm saying."

"So all that about the favor or pay-off—"

Lancaster grinned like the devil and looked twice as mean. "Bullshit. I'm going to break things on him. He's going to bleed. You know, when I'm done, he'll still be alive."

Terry nodded but was thinking Lancaster had stepped over the line, the one that he usually didn't mind toeing, no matter how close. From now on, Terry was second fiddle, a little like Crabtree. Somewhere along the way to Tampa, he needed to disappear and stay gone. But he knew he wouldn't. His stomach lurched and he tumbled out of bed.

"I don't feel too good man."

"Probably that sandwich meat."

Terry stumbled into the bathroom and flick on the light, shut the door. He squinted at the sudden brightness. He caught his breath. Sickness subsiding. Then he opened his eyes—hair in the sink, hair on the floor, a cheap razor on the back of the toilet. Blood was smeared on the tile, on the toilet, in the sink. More than a few nicks, it looked like Lancaster had gouged himself pretty bad. Terry remembered the dream. He turned on the shower, ice cold, and stuck his head under until he felt in control again, at least for a few moments.

He heard Lancaster through the door. "Hurry up so we can get out of here. I'm sick of this room."

NINETEEN

Lydia followed Alan into the bedroom, leaving Megan with Norm. He never found the strawberry water, so he fell back onto the couch, hands in his pockets, looking bored. Megan went over and sat near him, knees together and posture perfect.

She said, "Why are you looking for these two guys, anyway?"

"It's a long story." Norm shook his head. "I don't think I should tell you anyway."

"Why not?"

"It's not exactly legal."

They were quiet. Lydia and Alan talked in the bedroom, their voices not carrying. Norm couldn't keep his eyes off the little nurse when she looked away. He always blinked or turned elsewhere when her blank face turned to him. She slipped off a shoe, rubbed her foot up her leg, then crossed over her knee. She flexed a toe in the stocking and ran it down Norm's shin.

"I'll let you fuck me if you tell me the story," Megan said.

"You're lying."

"No, really. I want to know why you're chasing Lancaster and his friend. If you tell me, I will take off all my clothes and let you do whatever you want with me for a little while."

Norm laughed. He shifted around and couldn't keep his hands still. Megan's toe never stopped moving. She had cute little feet, Norm thought.

"How old are you?" He said.

"Twenty-two."

"You look younger. Can you prove it?"

Megan smiled, her cheeks like the girl from *Spider-Man*. It was the first Norm had seen from her, so tasty this way. She smelled really clean, all soap and no perfume. Norm's hand dropped to his lap.

Megan said, "I didn't bring ID. And who cares anyway? It's not like I'm going to tell. Don't I sound like you can trust me?"

Norm leaned towards her and whispered, "I don't have any condoms."

She whispered, "And?"

Norm liked her eyes and he couldn't get over the smell, Jesus, like pure pheromones, plus the toe and the stockings and her tight little body.

He told her, "It started when Alan bought his car."

Alan gathered the things Lydia would need from her bedroom—her pills, catheter bags, extra clothes—while she hovered nearby sighing and hoping he would catch the signal.

He did. "What's wrong?"

"Nothing, sweetie. Nothing."

"We don't have time for that." Alan sat down on the bed. Lydia puffed her straw, creeping closer until their knees touched. She felt terrible, scared, but was putting up a little act to look sad as well. Alan was so different, so in charge. She wanted to remind him who had made him that way.

"It's moving so fast," she said. "Where are we going and how long will we have to stay? All my money is tied up here, and they'll be tracing if I try to move it. We can't let Norm and that girl in on what we've got together."

Alan put his hands on her thighs, leaned forward and kissed her lips. It was soft and simple. He pulled away and she willed her plastic hands to reach for his. They didn't move.

"We'll lose Norm as soon as you want, if that's what you mean. He's going to cause problems, I can tell. He's a selfish prick."

Lydia nodded. "Let's, you know, get a little distance between us. Maybe when he falls asleep in the car."

"I was worried you were interested in keeping him around. Maybe my replacement."

"Him? You're joking, right? It's all business."

"Look at me, though. This is all right with you?" Alan pinched fat on his side.

"Have I ever done anything to make you think otherwise?"

He smiled. "Jesus, I love you."

"The nurse, I don't know. Maybe we can do them both at the same time."

"Do?"

"Alan, don't make me say it."

There was a flash of light outside the window along with engine noise. Someone pulling a car into the driveway. Alan went to the window and peeked out.

"Cops," he said, the old Alan breathing it out like he was already handcuffed.

Lydia stuck her emotions into deep freeze. "Get the other two. Here's what we do."

TWENTY

Half a minute after banging on the front door, the three officers and one detective were greeted by a cute college-age girl in an old nurse uniform, white stockings, and black loafers that looked too big for her.

"Can I help you?"

"We're looking for Lydia—" the detective checked his notepad, "Whipps."

"Come in and I'll get her."

The officers came in and spread out in search mode. The detective followed the girl out of the foyer into the living room, where Lydia sat in her chair waiting for them with a pleasant face.

"Miss Whipps?"

"Miss, sure. I'll take that. What's going on here."

"We need to have a talk. I'm Detective Broussard." He was a black man in his thirties built like a linebacker. Dark skin, fast eyes, and a deep Southern voice that weighed every word. "Did you rent a car recently?"

Lydia laughed and turned to Megan, who smiled in spite of pretending to tidy up the room. Lydia said, "My arms and legs are fake. I can't move them. My assistant does the driving, and for me that means a special van. I wish I could rent a car and just go away."

The detective laced his fingers under his chin. "Who did this to you?"

"The doctors. That was to save my life. See, it was a car accident. Why would you think someone would actually *do* this to me?"

"Well, your husband's murder—"

"You did your homework. So you also know he was my ex, and we weren't on good terms. He was a lying prick."

Broussard glanced at his notes again. "This rental car, your husband's name and address were given. The clerk doesn't remember because it was a busy day. Did your assistant rent it?" He nodded at Megan.

"She has her own car, never had problems with it. I'm sure she didn't."

Broussard sat on the edge of the couch near Lydia and spoke low. "Maybe she did it without telling you, you know? Identity theft, that sort of thing. It's a big fad right now, and in your condition..." He leaned back and made a noise like *Hmph?*

"You think so?"

"Could be. The problem is it wasn't her driving the car. Two guys, one fat, one kinda wiry looking." He held up a black and white security camera shot of Alan and Norm as they left the emergency room. "You know these guys?"

Lydia asked Megan to bring the photo closer. It was on copy paper, washed out and hard to see clearly. She did, holding it half an inch from Lydia's face. Broussard didn't like it, her face hidden from view like that.

Lydia's voice from behind the photo said, "No, I don't think I do. The little one looks familiar in a vague sort of way."

"So you do know him?"

"I said no. I was thinking aloud, that's all, trying to help."

Megan handed the photo back to Broussard, who moved it to the bottom of his pile. He handed another shot to Megan, grinning at her while he did. "Would you mind showing the lady this one, then, please?"

"I'm right here," Lydia said. "You can speak to me directly."

"Yes I know, but this one you're going to love."

The shot was of Megan in her white nurse's dress exiting the ER.

Broussard said, "She followed them out not even a minute later. Remember, these are stills from a video, so we can show you the whole thing if you prefer. They stole an ambulance, all three of them, and that ambulance is down the street. Maybe you should tell me what's really up here."

A gunshot blasted from outside the open window. Broussard had quick reflexes, moved so goddamn fast that the shot missed his head, skimmed his shoulder. He was on the floor shouting for help. Megan crouched behind Lydia's chair.

"Get out of my way, I can't steer," Lydia said.

One uniformed cop took cover behind the couch and drew down, firing out the window. He barked, "*Officer down! Officer down!*" into the handset on his shoulder.

Broussard pulled himself forward on his elbows infantry-style. Another shot from outside hit his thigh. He grunted and kept moving until he cleared the couch and rolled behind it, a smear of blood trailing him. "Where the fuck are the rest of you?" Broussard shouted at his cops.

Alan had sent Norm outside with a .38, told him to only use it in an emergency. He should have told the guy what he meant by that. He had knocked out the second cop nosing around the house, sneaked up behind him in the kitchen after leaving the first one in the guest bathroom, hoping to get all four and pile them in the ambulance before they woke up. Alan needed time, man, more time to get everything ready.

Moving someone in Lydia's condition wasn't a simple deal. She was worth the effort. Without her, he didn't have much to look forward to—more odd jobs, hanging around the edges of the underworld. He wanted respect, never found in the real world, where he'd made a mess of the nice jobs, or with criminals because he wasn't connected well enough and they thought he was a disgusting sweaty pig anyway. Lydia saw him differently, demanded more of him, made him feel wanted, and that had caused others see him with more respect, too.

Norm fucked it all up. They should've taken care of him much earlier. Then again, he wasn't the one who stumbled across Tompkins and Alan in the woods, either. Stumbled? No, Terry and Lancaster were in on this from the beginning. Norm was in on it with them, had to be.

So Alan knocked out this cop and everything was going fine when the shots exploded and scared Alan silly. He dropped to his knees behind the counter, one knee landing on the cop's chest, sounded like he cracked a rib. More shots, some yelling, Alan crazy wanting to know if Lydia was all right. He crawled around the counter, under the table, finally getting a decent angle to see into the living room. The detective rolled behind the couch, helped by the last uniform. No telling how many were outside or around the block already on their way.

Shit, shit, you little fuck, Norm. Not an emergency at all. Probably a tough question. What, he didn't think Lydia could handle tough questions from men? It was like a sixth sense for her now.

Alan guessed he had a couple of choices and not much time to consider either one. Commando his way into the living room guns blazing and make a beeline for the closest car, or take off out the back and run for his life, leaving Lydia to the cops and never looking back.

There was a third option that wasn't an option. Stay put, get caught, and plead for mercy. Alan wouldn't make it half a day in prison. Norm might last longer, only as a punk.

Before Ronnie and Cap and Lydia, the idea of anything but running was absurd. Alan Crabtree, brave? You kidding? He remembered the shock on Lancaster's face when he pulled the trigger on the woods. Relived the moment he yanked the ambulance driver out and tossed him like a kitten to the pavement. More than that, *felt* those moments all over again. The difference before Lydia and after was one thing—less fear.

He checked the pistols he had lifted from the cops, clicked the safeties off, made sure a round was chambered in each, and took a deep breath. He didn't want to fire until the last possible second, never giving the cops much of a target. He eased out from beneath the table and worked himself up like a bull aiming for the red cape.

Norm didn't want to hang out at the window anymore. He'd been hit in the hand by the cop's bullet and was going into shock. He lay on the grass outside for what felt like hours sucking in breaths and unable to cry. Not hours, though. More like minutes. Seconds? He sat up and lifted the bloody hand, a finger gone and another barely there, all of it purple and slick. It only hurt when he looked at it, nausea coming in waves.

He wrapped the hand in his shirt so it rested high on his stomach. He used the other hand to pull himself up, just in time to catch Alan exploding into the room, bullets from one pistol pounding away at the sofa. This was slow motion to Norm. Ten bullets super fast into the couch as Alan grabbed Lydia from her chair and hefted her over his shoulder. One of her legs went flying and her arms dangled mannequin-style. Alan dropped the empty pistol and grabbed another from his belt. More shots into the couch as he made a run for the front door, Megan crouching behind with her hands on her ears. When Alan was shield enough for her, she opened the door and yelled at him to hurry up. Alan and Lydia moved into the foyer. Then the door slammed.

All the noise shook Norm out of his stupor enough for him to stumble towards the front of the house. He made it in time to see Alan opening the garage door, Lydia still over his shoulder, now with only one arm, the other limbs on the porch. Norm felt drunk as he walked, barely able to keep his balance. The cop cars were empty, doors open and radios buzzing. His last few steps were strong, making it to the back passenger's door of the Monte Carlo while Alan placed Lydia in the front and strapped her in. She was bawling, not making words. Alan was gentle.

He noticed Norm trying to open the car door. He stood and aimed the pistol over the top of the car at Norm.

"Get away from us," Alan said.

"Your clip's empty."

"You counted all the bullets? You know for sure?"

"Empty." Norm looked down, made his free hand work the door handle. It clicked and he nudged it open, slipping into the car while the door banged his side. His clothes hung up. He didn't care because the bad hand was still bleeding and he wanted to sleep.

Lydia saw him in the rearview mirror. "Oh God, Norm. What's that?"

"My hand." The words slurred like a tape getting eaten. He pointed to his shirt balled tight around his hand. Megan kept far away, pressing against the opposite door.

Alan walked around and leaned into Norm's face.

"I said emergencies only. You don't know what the fuck that means, or you just like playing with guns. I ought to kill you." Alan looked at the hand. "Looks like you'll be dying slowly anyway."

He shut the door hard, ran around to shut Lydia's. She was staring at the lone arm on her lap.

"Get it off me," she told Alan.

"You don't want it? Better than nothing."

"*Get it off, get it off! Off!*" She bawled like a kid, and Alan fumbled with the straps until it was free and he tossed it to the side. Lydia calmed down.

"It was mocking me, only having one. Thought I was back in the crash," she said.

"It's fine. See? Gone."

"It's not fair," she whispered.

Alan closed her door gently.

Once on the road, they had nowhere to go. Norm fell asleep. No one tried to wake him. They listened to be sure he was still breathing.

"We can't keep driving," Megan said.

Alan shook his head.

"So?"

He raised his shoulders and held them up a long time before he drooped and sighed enough to fog his side of the windshield. "I don't know."

TWENTY-ONE

Terry and Lancaster sat on the beach in Biloxi drinking beer while they talked about how to find and kill Alan Crabtree. They were in the tern nest areas, supposed to be off-limits—tall grass shielded them from the passers-by on the highway that ran along the beach. The sun was setting, the orange glow purpling up the clouds, Terry listening to a terrible plan about offering to hire Crabtree, getting word out through the underground, and then killing him when he comes to see about the job.

"It won't work. He's probably done with killing," Terry said.

"We've guessed wrong about him plenty the last few days."

Terry cupped sand in his palm and let fall between his fingers.

Lancaster was strengthening faster than Terry imagined, almost as if he didn't have major surgery only hours before, and his revenge plan was all he talked about. When Terry didn't agree or at least nod or something, Lancaster would bark or punch him on the arm. Strange how a man with his main arm in a sling could be such a good punch with the other. Boxing training, had to be. Terry had always assumed it was natural.

Lancaster finished the bottle of Busch and stuck it deep in the sand, bottom end up. It was his third. Terry sipped along on his first, ignored how warm and lifeless it was.

"You have a better plan? Maybe some complicated shit I'd need to have a degree to get right?" Lancaster said.

"It's not that. He'll be careful next time is what I'm saying. You need to surprise him."

"What's not a surprise about this? He shows up expecting a client, and it's us. Bammo, he's dead. Surprise, fucking surprise, fuck you. I don't get you anymore." Lancaster rolled his eyes and shook his head. He reached behind him for the shopping bag full of beer and pulled out his fourth. He twisted the cap with his teeth easily, then spit it in the sand. Terry saw dots of blood surrounding Lancaster's pile of caps. He was on revenge overdrive, no pain or shit. Scared Terry silly.

"He doesn't have a lot of friends. You need to find his friends and that's how you can get him." Terry was careful to say *you* instead of *we*, hoping the guy would catch on. Lancaster was too wrapped up to really listen. "Did you hear me?"

"Sure, yeah. Find his friends. I'm not after the friends."

Terry wanted to shake his head and yell, *You never listen, you dumb ass muscle boy*. Instead, he cupped more sand. The deeper he dug, the more wet the sand. The white dusty stuff kept falling back into the hole. Terry didn't like being outside. The gnats buzzed around his ears and nose, biting his arms and face.

"I want one of those girls," Lancaster said.

Terry looked up. "Show me."

Lancaster pointed at a group of high-schoolers—they looked sixteen, seventeen, three girls and a couple of guys hanging out in a pickup truck by the seawall, all in swimsuits and shirts, the girls squeaking and laughing like it was the best day of their lives.

"Jesus, man, they're kids."

"They're not kids. Look at their hair, and they leave those cut off shorts unzipped. Shit, they want it."

"We can find girls at the bar."

"I don't want bar girls. I want one of those." He pushed himself off the sand. "Come on, we can act like we'll buy them beer or something, then get rid of the guys, then take us a couple girls."

Terry felt weak all over. He liked the short girl who looked latina, but he didn't like where this was going at all. These were kids. You scammed them, sometimes fucked them if they wanted it. You never just *took* them.

"Man," Terry said.

"Shut the fuck up and look cool. I need you to help anyway. I can't hold her down with only one arm."

In the hotel room later, the door slammed and Terry and Lancaster were left alone. Terry held a pillow to his chest and shivered while Lancaster wiped blood off his dick with a towel.

"Goddamn virgin," he mumbled.

What happened was they had talked to these kids and offered them beer. The teens were suspicious at first, a heavyset girl saying something about being from a Methodist youth group. The guys were quiet, waiting for an excuse to make threats, their arms crossed and muscles tensed. Frat guys, Terry knew without a doubt, like he once was, and they were hanging with underage girls. Typical. A couple of years of that frat lifestyle, barely passing school, too much beer and not enough upkeep, all of the sudden Terry was twenty-nine and flabby, running cons instead of practicing law like his dad hoped he would.

Lancaster shrugged at the kids, the supposed holy rollers, and said, "That hip hop stuff you're listening to, that's not some Christian band, is it? Sounds like Nelly to me."

"It's only music."

"Music about fucking, that's what it is. Take a beer." He held the bag out to the guys, who stayed rock still. The latina girl stepped between the bag and the tough boy. She reached in and took a bottle, held it out to Lancaster.

"Open it for me?"

Lancaster grinned and did the thing with his teeth. The girl smiled.

Another girl, taller and skinnier with punk blonde hair, the one Lancaster really wanted, took another bottle and said, "We're just partying, letting off steam."

The guys calmed down and took beer, still quiet, more because they knew Lancaster overtook Alpha Male status. Terry gave up on the latina, who ignored him, but the heavyset girl wanted to talk. She wasn't awful, had a very pretty face, and acted older, like a college girl. Probably a senior in high school, though, or a dropout.

Lancaster asked if they could borrow the truck to get more beer. The skinny girl asked for Zima. He left the latina girl and the guys, told Terry to drive. The heavy girl climbed into the truck bed. The skinny girl sat on Lancaster's lap.

The girls were obviously afraid when Terry pulled into the hotel parking lot after getting the booze. They tried playing it tough.

"Shit, you better buy me dinner first," the heavyset girl said.

Terry grinned, helped her out of the truck. "We're picking up something. Only be a few minutes." The lie sounded too bright coming out of his mouth.

In the room, the heavyset girl said she had to pee and headed for the bathroom. The skinny girl sat on the edge of the bed and crossed her legs. A big mistake, Terry thought. *Run, please, run, don't do this, please.*

Lancaster sat beside her and they started making out. Terry tried not to watch, turning the TV on and clicking to VH1. The smacking was loud and it was a small room. The girl didn't know how to kiss and Lancaster didn't care. His free hand was all over her, and she didn't mind—fingers on her back, her ass, her breasts, all with a breathy "Oh yeah." When Lancaster tried to get the cutoff shorts out of the way, she fought back.

"No, slow down, man. Come on, we're just having fun," she said. The voice was young.

The toilet flushed and the heavyset girl came out of the bathroom shaking her hair and giggling at Lancaster and her friend until she saw the struggle.

"That's not cool," she said.

Terry said, "It's nothing."

The skinny girl saw her friend and started to say, "Help—"

Lancaster covered her mouth with his lips, the weight of his cast pinning her stomach and one arm. The shorts were down to her knees, then slipped to her ankles.

"See, she's into it," Terry said.

The heavy girl grabbed Terry's arm and said, "You need to stop him. This is wrong now. You're not like him, so you can stop him."

VH1 blared one of those shows that talked about videos instead of playing them, so Terry kept hearing clips of Quiet Riot in the background between interviews.

"Let them go, okay? You and me, wanna take a shower?" Terry said.

The girl looked repulsed. It was pure, unexpected, no-doubt repulsion.

Lancaster was having trouble with the bikini bottoms. "Hey, a little help, my man."

Terry took a step forward, glanced back at the larger girl, then shrugged at her. He turned to Lancaster. "What do you need?"

"Whatever you can do. Slip a finger in and yank them off, man. Then get her arms."

The big girl grabbed Terry from behind and pulled him away. He got free, but her fingernails had cut him. "Shit, leave me alone, okay? Go sit down or join in."

"*Get off her,*" the big girl yelled.

"Shit, do something with her," Lancaster said. "Then help me."

Terry shoved the big girl over the empty bed. She tumbled and came back up ready to fight. Terry opened the drawer with the Bible and picked up the steak knife he stashed there. They didn't have guns, but he needed something, especially for his own protection against Lancaster. He held it towards the big girl, who slumped into the tight corner between the bed and the wall.

"Terry, now," Lancaster said.

Why the fuck give them a name? Even the fake one?

Terry pulled the skinny girl's bikini bottom and sliced it with the knife. They came off one leg, and he pulled it down. The girl had some hair down there, though not much, and Terry almost cut Lancaster. He could do it—the neck, the chest, the stomach. He could do it.

He didn't do it.

Lancaster worked his own shorts down, throbbing dick looking for a place to find relief. Terry grabbed the girl's flailing arms by the wrists and pinned them. Her face was tear-streaked and she looked Terry in the eye and said, "Please don't. Please. I'm only sixteen."

Lancaster grunted. "Most girls start when they're sixteen."

"Not like this, please. No."

Lancaster pressed her thighs open and found what he was looking for. The girl's eyes went wide and she sucked in air, let it out in small hurtful sounds. Terry turned his head. The other girl was crying, too. She seemed paralyzed on the other side of the bed. Terry watched the heavyset girl watching her friend being raped.

Then they left fast without a word and took off in the truck. Lancaster wiped the girl's blood from his dick and pulled off the stained sheets. The blood soaked through to the mattress.

Lancaster grinned. "Fuck. I didn't think I lasted long enough for it to soak through."

Terry rocked back and forth. "They'll tell the cops. We need to get the hell out of here."

"Yeah, I know. Still got a few minutes. Let me get my clothes on. Pack your shit. Man, we've got DNA all over this room. Too bad we're not done in town."

"Not done? We're done. We can't stay here now, are you nuts? Trying to lay low, want to find Crabtree, and you fucking *rape* a girl? What's wrong with you?"

Lancaster dropped the sheets to the floor and frowned at Terry. What an evil goddamn expression. "You calling it rape now?"

"Don't start with me."

"No, answer the question, *dear*. Rape? You say that was rape?"

Terry nodded but turned his eyes away. "Yeah, I guess."

Lancaster bolted towards Terry and grabbed the pillow, tossed it across the room. Terry held his palms out keeping Lancaster away. The guy slapped them down and banged Terry upside the head with his cast. Lancaster balled his good hand and punched Terry's face. Terry felt things crack and burn. Only a few punches, but Terry wanted to pass out. He covered his face, felt wetness. He looked down into blood and salt water. Cuts over his eye, on his cheek, maybe a cracked bone.

Lancaster backed off, reached down for the sheets. He said, "Whatever you call it, you helped me, bitch."

TWENTY-TWO

The drive from Biloxi to New Orleans took just over an hour. Alan thought it was a good place to start "getting lost." It wasn't a really big city as much as it was crowded, usually packed with tourists. He found a packed hotel near the airport and took a room. Hopefully the four of them could slip in without being noticed since it was one of those hotels where the rooms were all accessible from the parking lot. A nice ground floor room in the back, a place to count blessings and decide where to go from there.

The world was open to them—an airport next door if they could make a flight before the cops sent out an all points bulletin, plenty of cash from cleaning out one of Lydia's checking accounts at a gas station ATM. On the way over, with the car speakers turned to the back so he could have some privacy, he asked Lydia, "Where do you want to go?"

She barely moved her lips when she said, "Home."

"Really, sweetie. Have you thought about it?"

She turned her head to him, eyes full of surrender. Strapped into the seat without her rubber arms and legs, it was like she had lost the real ones all over again, and her plans for ruling Norm's little empire were ruined. "Wherever you choose, it's fine. I don't really care."

"I was thinking New Mexico for some reason. I don't know why. Hell, *old* Mexico is just as good. We've got passports, right?"

"Did you get mine?"

"I think so. Still, from New Mexico we can drive down if we want. I want to see Cabo. Sammy Hagar's got a club there, loves the place. *Cabo Wabo.*"

At the hotel, he parked in front of the room and got out. He took Lydia in first and situated her on one of the beds.

"You need to pee first, something like that?"

She shook her head.

Alan lingered a moment, hands in his pockets. This wasn't like Lydia to be so quiet. He needed her to lead. Up to that moment he was improvising, guessing what she would do, waiting for some guidance that never came. He wanted her to tell him *what to do*.

"Did you kill those cops?" she said.

Alan shrugged. "Not the first two. The guys in the living room, I don't even know. I aimed low at the couch, tried to scare them."

She grinned faintly, enough to let him know it was the right thing to do. "I'll be right back," he said.

Megan and Norm were both asleep. She was easy to wake up. Alan struggled with Norm, hand still wrapped in his shirt, beginning to stink, finally shaking the man conscious enough to stand up. Alan nearly carried him inside, placed him sitting up in the tub. It might be the place he would die. Standing over Norm, Alan blamed him for everything and worried about him at the same time. It was like Lydia was The Wizard all this time and his newfound boldness was an illusion. With her down, he was Cowardly Lion again.

He knelt by the tub and lifted Norm's wrapped hand, worked the shirt free with delicate fingering, the blood drying like glue but still tacky. When finished, Alan stared at the leftover pulp that used to be a hand. A bullet must have struck between the fingers and ripped straight through. The thumb was barely there. The pinkie, black and purple, swollen. Norm was too far gone to feel Alan as he turned the wrist gently to see all the way around.

A voice at his ear said, "Oh my God."

Alan swung his head, almost bumping Megan in the nose. She was right over his shoulder. He didn't hear her come into the bathroom.

"Is he going to be all right?" she said.

"I don't know. It might heal up, it might get infected, probably get infected. He's been in shock for a while, too. I can pour some peroxide on it, I guess."

"That might hurt him."

"Look at his goddamn hand, honey. What can be worse? Either I try a little something or we give up and pray over him. Other than that, what else can we do?"

She crossed her arms and stood straight. The innocent act was wearing thin. Alan didn't know what to make of her pouring on the flirt with him. Same act she pulled on Norm right before the cops knocked on the door, catching her rubbing all over him when they showed up at Lydia's, about one base away from a homer.

"I didn't know this would happen. I'm so sorry. It's all my fault, because if I hadn't come along, you might've have had more time," she said.

Alan nodded. "You're right."

Her face went hard fast as flicking a switch. "Well, it's too late. I'm here for the rest of the ride, so get used to it. I can help your leper girlfriend in there when you're not around."

Alan stood and shoved Megan against the wall. "You won't call her names. You'll treat her with respect, and if I find out you don't, maybe you're not as hard to get rid of as you think."

Megan slipped down and crawled between Alan's legs. He tried to close them around her waist. She twisted through and sat up by the tub, running her hand through Norm's hair. "Poor guy. And the things he told me right before we were interrupted, you wouldn't believe." She clucked her tongue and closed her eyes.

Alan thought of ten things to say, finally not saying any of them. He turned and walked out of the bathroom.

Lydia was having trouble sorting awake from dreaming. It happened often the past several years but she always had the prosthetic arms and legs to bring her back to earth, keep her grounded. Without them her daydreams overloaded her brain, and even with her eyes open she wasn't seeing the claustrophobic hotel room with the smell of orange-scented deodorizer. She was standing at the door, walking out. She was in the lobby of the hotel asking the desk clerk to call her a cab.

When Alan carried Norm into the room and to the bathroom, Lydia's thoughts were far away, the taxi ride only a few seconds like a TV show edit, back at her home in Biloxi, no blood or dead policemen. She sat on her couch and watched those curtains ripple liquid in the breeze. That was peaceful, the only thing that really smothered her anger.

Megan lumbered into the hotel room, stood over Lydia's bed with crossed arms and stared at her a moment before heading for the bathroom. It only registered far back in Lydia's subconscious mind. The girl was from another time and place and Lydia had moved on.

The phone ringing in her home. Ronnie apologizing. Lydia's hand ached a little from holding the phone to her ear but it was okay. Ronnie was sad, missing Lydia while he rotted in the grave. So sorry to have been blind to her beauty, grace, and calm. She answered, "I know, it's okay. I accept. I'm so glad you called." Ronnie told her God had forgiven him and he was going to be let into Heaven when the time came. She was happy for him. Then an invisible boulder sat beside her on the couch, sank into the cushion. An invisible paw stroked her hair. She batted at it with her hands but they felt nothing.

The orange fumes burned like smelling salts and Lydia jerked her head, blinking fast, flailing hands that weren't there, but the aching still was. Alan sat on the bed with her, brushing his fingers through her hair. The lights made everything in the room look bigger.

"Are you all right?" Alan said.

"I can't stay this way. You can't carry me around in a sack or over your shoulder."

"I know."

"Then where can we get a wheelchair? And keeping the prosthetics would've been nice."

"We didn't have time, sweetie. And you didn't want the one that was left."

Lydia turned to the curtains, bland and heavy and hiding the window. The only way to regain control was pretend she never lost it. "Going back to Biloxi isn't an option. We need to leave soon."

"Okay. Have you decided on a place yet?"

"Anywhere warm with a direct flight tonight will be fine. We can start there until I'm ready to move again."

Alan nodded. "They'll find us. Running around like this is all silly, but it's the best we've got. Maybe Mexico will swallow us and no one will ever bother looking for us anymore. I only killed one man, after all."

"Two men. Cap, remember? And you tried to kill Lancaster. And you're about to kill Norm, am I right?"

Alan didn't say anything. He sighed and dropped his fat chin, looking more and more like the shaky blob who showed up at her house one afternoon a couple months before, no backbone and afraid of his own shadow.

"Alan?"

"It's not like he's going to live much longer anyway. Really, his hand is a mess and he's in shock, and if we sit here a while then nature will take care of it for us, but God knows when. Shit, this girl, she wants to go with us. I don't know what to do."

"We might need Norm to help us with contacts."

"Didn't Ronnie have contacts?"

"That's ancient history. We need who Norm knows." Lydia's eyes did a Bette Davis thing before she said, "Put me in the chair."

Alan lifted her from the bed, cradling her like an infant as he carried her around the bed to one of the two plush chairs. He eased her down and then knelt in front of the chair, hands gripping the armrests, ready to catch Lydia if she fell. Lydia lifted her chin, so Alan leaned his ear close to her mouth.

"Where is she?"

Alan said, "In the bathroom with Norm."

"She's listening," Lydia said, mumbling. It was easier to hear whispering from a distance than mumbling, she thought. Alan nodded his understanding.

Lydia went on. "Tell her she can come. Keep telling her until we're ready. You need to be strong for me and end her for me when I ask you too. Don't you hate the way she looks at me? Like she wants to take my place. What can *she* do for you better than me?"

"Nothing," Alan mumbled.

"She doesn't care about you like I do. You believe I care, right? This whole time we've been together—"

"I know, sweetie. You've shown it everyday."

Megan appeared in the bathroom door, a frown on her face.

"Kiss me," Lydia said.

Alan kissed her, a needy kiss that she tried to return with equal energy. She closed her eyes a moment, then fluttered them open to watch Megan's frown crimp into disgust before she turned to the door and walked out to the parking lot.

Lydia allowed Alan to keep kissing her after she was ready for it to stop. Let him take what he needs, she thought. Fill him up like a camel.

Megan sat on the bathroom floor after Crabtree left trying to think of how to get to Lancaster before these people could kill him. She needed more information about him and his friend, more than these liars were giving her.

Until meeting Lancaster, Megan had nothing in life that really compelled her—it was the same every day, no reason to wake up.

Then Megan saw this man who was exactly like the man she daydreamed about when imagining The One. The relationship that would change her life by making her feel alive and passionate and lustful and damn-near-anything again. It was this guy, the one with the bloody arm and the muscles and the square jaw.

The fire alarm scattered everyone and she lost track except for seeing Crabtree go after a minivan. She was glad she paid attention.

She almost had more info from Norm, him ready to spill everything he knew for a chance to fuck her. So so close. Then the cops showed up and everyone scrambled and Norm got shot and these other two weren't going to tell her a damn thing.

She glanced at Norm, still dead to the world in the tub. Megan reached behind her for a towel hanging from the rack, pulled it down and spread it over Norm so she wouldn't have to look at that hand. All that about feeling sorry for Norm and wanting to get him some help—it wasn't all false. She felt sorry for him.

Killing him now would probably be a good idea, though, if she wanted Crabtree and Lydia to consider taking her along. It would make things more urgent. She glanced around the bathroom, looking for something sharp. It was a typical bare bones hotel bathroom, round edges and everything screwed tightly. She still had the paper from the cop's pad out there in her nurse's uniform, one of the pockets. Even if Lancaster's friend lied and gave a false address and number, calling it wouldn't hurt anyone.

Megan pushed herself up the wall until she was standing. She heard low talking in the main room, unable to make out any words. She peeked out and saw Crabtree on his knees in front of Lydia, now sitting up in the chair, more circus freaky than ever. Lydia watched Megan a moment over Crabtree's shoulder, then said something to him. He leaned in for a kiss.

Megan felt nauseous.

In the car she found the paper with the phone number, smoothed it out on the seat. It was hard to read in the dark, so she climbed out and found a good spot near the streetlight. The number had a 601 area code, not a Coast number, not a local call, probably a pizza joint or something at random. At least it gave her something to do besides sit in there with The Human Blob and the Limbless Lady. She needed to hurry before Crabtree came looking.

Megan went back to the car and found a quarter under the driver's seat, along with old French fries and dried lettuce strips. She found a dime in the ashtray and hoped pay phone prices hadn't risen since the last time she used one. There was one by the streetlight, next to the fence separating the hotel parking lot from the nearly abandoned shopping center next door full of nameless marquees and boarded doors. She looked back at the room, no one peeking through the curtains yet, then hightailed it to the phone.

She dropped the money in and dialed collect. The electronic operator asked her to say her name at the tone, something those guys wouldn't know, so Megan slammed in, "I need to talk to Lancaster" before it cut off. Then the voice told her to wait while they connected. Whether the person on the other end accepted or not, at least it would answer *one* question, Megan thought.

TWENTY-THREE

Lancaster told Terry the pros and cons of fucking virgins—less chance for disease, more chance the girl would be a boring lay.

Terry said, "What if she had AIDS because her Mom did when she was born, or some blood transfusion? Or hepatitis from a mosquito?"

"I said *less* chance, not none. And what the hell is life without risk anyway? You're a fuck. I see now how you are, talking your way out of shit to stay safe. That's not as cool as I used to think it was."

Terry's face was swelled and he held ice in a cloth to his face. Stung like hell. Lancaster hadn't said another word about it. Terry sat in the chair and stared at TV. Lancaster even started telling him what he could and couldn't watch—"No more dating shows, fucking game shows, man. Get us some music. We got music? I want BET or something."

So Terry suffered through ten minutes of *Rap City* while Lancaster got dressed. He thought Lancaster was more into Motorhead or AC/DC. Terry glanced at his watch again. Lancaster was acting like he was getting ready for a night out in the clubs rather than a fucking escape. The scarred bald scalp was freaky enough without the guy was primping shirtless in front of the mirror.

Then Terry's cell phone rang.

"I thought you got rid of that thing," Lancaster said.

"I got rid of the last one. This one I took off Tompkins. I needed something, you know, in case I went for a burger and your doctor wanted me."

Lancaster whipped his head around and turned sinister. "You *gave* a doctor a *real fucking number?*"

Terry shrugged. Third ring on the phone. He flipped the cover while saying, "I forgot I had it after we left the hospital. I thought it was temporary."

"Maybe the doctor remembered and gave it to the cops."

"I should answer it."

"Why?"

A shrug. "Don't you want to know for sure?"

"I don't care. You shouldn't care. They'll trap us, buddy. It's all their game plan."

Terry pressed the talk button and said hello. The voice on the other end spoke. Terry blinked, a little shocked, and pointed at Lancaster. "Yeah, sure."

He listened another moment, then said, "Hold on."

Terry brought the phone to Lancaster and said, "It's for you. A girl."

Lancaster took the phone and grunted into it. He listened to the girl on the other end. He said, "I remember."

A couple of minutes later he said, "You hold tight, then. See if you can—well, stall them, then. I don't care. No, I care, but you do what's best."

Lancaster closed the phone and tossed it on the floor. "Crabtree's in New Orleans. He might be trying to fly out of there."

"How do you know that?"

"She told me."

"Who's she," Terry said.

Lancaster shook his head, bared his teeth and sucked air. The he said, "She says she was in the ER with me, a nurse in a white dress. I remember her. I swore she was an angel or something. She touched me, made the pain go away. That's crazy, right?"

Terry picked up the cell phone. "I saw her too, man. She came to the waiting room and told me you were going to be all right. I was half asleep, thought I was dreaming."

Lancaster stood and walked to the dresser. He pressed his fingertips on the mirror, leaned over until his cheek touched the glass. Terry watched without expression or words. Lancaster closed his eyes and breathed through his mouth so loud. "Had to be an angel," he whispered.

"It's a little convenient. Maybe that's part of that trap you were talking about," Terry said. "How did she get the number?"

Lancaster pushed off the mirror and paced the floor. "She *knows* things, man. I believe her. Can't explain it."

"Shit, you were doped up, I was half asleep. Maybe she's the bait, an undercover cop or something."

Lancaster came hard at Terry and shoved him to the floor. "You don't talk about her like that!"

"We need to be careful, that's all." Terry propped himself up. His back hurt. "Can't you stop for a minute? I'm not the one you want to kill, so ease up, man."

Lancaster leaned over and grabbed Terry's shirt. "What? I didn't hear that. Maybe I'm losing my hearing, but I didn't hear you."

Someone knocked like thunder on the door along with muffled shouts of "*Police.*"

Lancaster dropped Terry. "Look at that. Now you go and make us late so we have to face this bullshit."

"Hey, I told you—"

"How am I gonna kill cops with only one arm?"

Terry got his legs moving and stood. He said, "Let me talk to them. We can find a way out of all this."

"You've talked enough. That trooper would've hauled us in if I hadn't shot him. Get in the bathroom and listen, do what I say, you dig?"

Terry sprinted to the bathroom, turned off the light and hid behind the door. He closed his eyes. He didn't want to see anything, not even shadows, so he squeezed his eyes until the blackness turned green and then black again.

Lancaster opened the door to find what he expected—two cops, guns drawn and held at their sides, slightly back, trigger fingers straight on the guard. The lead cop was bulky, obvious weightlifter, no sideburns. The one behind him was a bit sunburned. Young, too. Lancaster thought, *They're sending rookies after rapists now? No respect.*

The cops inched forward, not wanting to risk getting too close and being surprised. "What's going on here?"

"Excuse me?"

"You having some problems? Step back."

Lancaster did, and the cops came inside. The sunburned cop looked around. "Where's your friend?"

"He's getting some burgers. How did you know about him? I don't get this."

The sunburned cop checked under the beds, then was about to check the bathroom when Lancaster tripped and caught the big cop's shirt going down, managed to sit on the bed. The cop pulled loose and swung the gun around.

Lancaster held up his free hand, winced. "Okay, it's okay. I'm still off-balance with this cast. Sorry."

"You been busy lately? Smells like fucking in here."

"Look—"

"Some girls? Young girls?" He pointed to the bare mattress.

Lancaster looked up. "This is crazy. I can't even dress myself."

"Your friend helped. We'll need to straighten this out." The cop pulled out his cuffs. "I can loop this around your cast strap, maybe."

The younger cop edged closer to the bathroom door. Lancaster shook his head at the big cop, hoped he could time this right. "I really need to keep it like this, you know. Keep the pressure the way the doctor wants it."

The cop stood quiet a moment before he slipped the cuffs back in their case. It was what Lancaster wanted—the guy taking an inventory, then believing the girls might be lying. His bored face said he didn't trust women, so he eased up a little.

Lancaster exploded. He stuck his leg out in front of the cop and slammed the cast against the guy's back. The cop was falling to his knees, so Lancaster kicked the gun away and then kicked him in the nose.

The sunburned cop was near the bathroom door when he heard his partner grunt. He spun, enough to put him off-balance when Terry slammed the door into him and knocked him down. Lancaster brought a knee down hard on the big cop's neck. He reached over for the gun, on his opposite side, life or death Twister suddenly. Then the pistol was in his hand and shot without taking time to think. One in the big cops head, two at the cop across the room.

"Jesus, you could've hit me!" Terry yelled. He came out of hiding and found the other gun. "Like, you didn't even give me a chance. You'd wanted to kill me."

"You want to be dead, I can do it for you, the more you talk about it. Shut up and let's go."

Lancaster was sure another cruiser would be on the way, these two acting macho being closest to the call and not waiting. All they heard was "man in a cast" and they probably smirked, made a couple jokes, and headed over pretty quickly. Heroes, like on *Cops*. Lancaster kicked the big cop's ear.

"Get in the van," Terry said.

"Why not their car?"

"Sure, and let's paint targets on our heads and go on live TV. We can ditch the van and get something else down the road. Switching a few will throw them off."

"We're running out of time. The girl said Crabtree's leaving tonight."

Terry shook his head and sighed. He felt in charge again because Lancaster needed his help. He would never say it, but Terry knew that tone of voice. On his own, Lancaster would be dead within ten miles, dying in a blaze of glory bloodbath.

"You want to get Crabtree, we do it my way. You want to spend time fucking with more cops, *you* drive the cruiser. God knows we'll have enough cops to deal with before we're done."

Lancaster grinned at his partner. "See, why would I want to kill you?"

TWENTY-FOUR

Megan walked back to the room as a jet roared in for a landing, coming low over the parking lot, the hotel across the street from the runway. The jet fumes were strong and Megan held her breath while watching the plane set down, lights blinking on the wingtips. She had never flown on an airplane, never even been that close to one. Crabtree and Lydia wanted to ditch her and fly away, so Megan needed to make herself valuable, if only pretending.

She slipped into the room. Lydia sat on her throne, back to her ice queen demeanor, held upright with a couple of towels tied together around the chair. The woman stared at Megan with a smooth grin, not subtle at all. *Jesus*, Megan thought, *did she learn all her moves from soap operas?*

The bathroom light was on. She caught a reflection of Crabtree's back in the mirror, facing the tub. Megan pushed her way in, squeezed between Crabtree and Norm. Crabtree's gun dangled in his right hand, loose but ready.

"What are you doing? You're not going to shoot him in a hotel." Megan stroked Norm's greasy hair.

Crabtree shook his head and curled his lips like he was thinking hard. "No, not going to shoot him. Have to do something, though."

"What's with the gun, then?"

"I like holding it."

Megan nodded. "Let me sit with him a while. We could, I don't know, drown him? Fill up the tub slowly, let him slip under. I can chop up Lydia's muscle relaxers, too, mix them in water and pour it down him."

"Didn't have time to grab them. I don't have much that'll work."

Norm's breath was wheezy, same strength as it was an hour ago. Megan was beginning to think he wouldn't die easily. If there were a chance he could get up to speed again—

Those were all back-up plans, she remembered. Lancaster was on his way right at that moment, hurrying to be with her and take her away to a free life, no begging or borrowing. He would teach her to take what she wanted whenever she wanted it, give her anything she demanded, needed, *craved*. Megan daydreamed of a sailboat in the Gulf of Mexico, no land in sight, only she and Lancaster, sailing to Cuba, the Virgin Islands, and then the middle of nowhere.

"I've got some pills from the hospital. Maybe they'll work."

Crabtree wrinkled his face like something smelled bad, then said, "Maybe that's a good idea."

"Go reserve your tickets. I'll stay with Norm," she said.

"Gotta pay cash, so I guess I'll do it in person."

"Look, they don't let you on airplanes these days if you do suspicious stuff, so you have to put a card up at some point. ID, all that. And you can't take a gun."

"How do you know?"

"I watch TV. I know about the terrorist stuff. Shit, I still have my license right here." She patted her chest. "Stuck it in my bra. I'm not stupid. Show an ID, for the most part they'll leave you alone. If not, hit them in the face."

Crabtree smiled and grunted. "Like I need advice from you."

"What's your plan? Pull out a wad and say, 'Give me a ticket to anywhere, fast, no questions, please'?"

Crabtree backed out of the room. Megan sat on the edge of the tub and stared at the redneck's face. He didn't know what he was getting into. It was all Lydia's fault, pushing Norm to kill his partner when all he wanted to do was let off steam, at the most scare Tompkins, give him something to think about. That's what Norm told Megan right before the cops showed up at the house. Maybe he was telling her the truth or shading it in hindsight—overall, though, he didn't seem all that dishonest. Norm really wanted someone to talk to, and Megan was there, being sweet and sexy like fake-schoolgirl porn. He couldn't help it.

So he ended up in a tub with half a hand, probably infected by now, and in deep shock. Megan hated to see him that way, but didn't want to be helpless and pitiful like him ever again. She reached over and turned on the water, mixing it comfortably hot, and reached into her pockets for a handful of pill packets. She wanted to cry as she put them on the floor and crushed them under her heel.

Opened the plastic, dribbled a little warm water into them, and one by one slid the wet paste into Norm's mouth.

Norm was in the place where he thought his dream was real, a continuation of the life he was living, as if he hadn't been shot and if he kissed Megan and took her to his truck and made love to her, then started driving, just driving. Somehow he ended up on the dock of a fishing camp on a serene lake. *His* camp, the way he always pictured it, *his* boat tied to the dock, the big log cabin barely visible down the path up the hill. Megan was there in a sundress, her hair red for some reason, and she was barefoot, sipping a Pepsi from an old glass bottle. The sun cast a hazy calmness like a painting. The only thing missing was physical sensation. Why wasn't it warm? Why didn't he squint at the dazzle reflecting off the water? Why wasn't his dick getting hard looking at Megan's nipples visible through the thin dress? Hell, that would happen no matter what, he thought. Something was wrong.

Then he was warm. Slow, gradual, at his feet. He looked down to see the lake water rising quickly, over the dock, up his ankles, his shins. Megan floated, swam, her body completely visible as if she were naked. The water kept rising—knees, thighs, waist. Norm wanted to swim after Megan but he was frozen. Muscles didn't work. Chest, neck. He was still warming up, feeling wetness heavy like slime on his skin. He wanted to breath and breath deep before the water filled his mouth and nose and lungs, damn it, *breath in now, breath in now....*

Numb, and then nothing.

Norm's head barely thrashed after Megan turned off the water and pressed his head beneath the surface. When he was completely still, she waited several long minutes before draining the water. She watched his chest for movement, felt pretty sure he was dead.

She took Norm's cheeks in her hands and turned his face to hers. She reached her lips to his and kissed him. He was still warm.

Alan sat on the bed and stared at his shoes. Lydia sighed a few times trying to get his attention, and he knew that's why she did it, so he ignored her.

She finally said, "Please, what's wrong?"

He shrugged. "Nothing's wrong, really. I need some quiet to figure things out."

"I can help you."

I don't want your help, he thought. Until a couple of hours back, Alan had been grateful to her for toughening him up, giving him a spine. He saw it differently at that moment on the hotel, Megan scheming in the bathroom, Lydia more like furniture than his lover. She had never really expected him to stand on his own, right? *She* would make the plans. *She* would choose the targets. Alan shook his head. Not anymore.

To keep her from being suspicious, he went ahead and told her what was on his mind. "Catching a plane now probably isn't possible. Cops will be looking for us, plus we need a credit card to get tickets if we don't want anyone looking at us funny, and once we do it, we're traced."

"Use the goddamn credit card, then. We didn't come this far to stay here."

So fucking easy, isn't it? Always so easy when you don't do the thing yourself. Alan grinned and coughed to cover a laugh. "We'd have to move fast, soon as I buy the tickets. By the time we land, someone will probably already know. Listen, why not drive instead?"

"Sure, why not? That's a sure way to get to paradise quickly. We're maybe twelve hours from Mexico by car, only three by plane. Let's see—what's the better option? You need to count on your fingers?"

"Why don't you shut the fuck up?" Alan said.

Lydia didn't answer. Alan lifted his head to find her staring, hard-assed like a dominatrix about to whip him. Usually it scared him. It was how she got him into this mess with Norm anyway, cowing him with bitchiness. This time he turned his face to the TV.

"Look at me," Lydia said.

Alan stood and slapped her face. Nothing too serious, enough to shock her. They'd had rough sex, sure, but before this he never hurt her in anger.

Her mouth hung open, lips tremoring.

He leaned close. "Let me handle this one, okay? No fighting, no insulting, no nothing. I'll get us somewhere safe. I fucking love you, so trust me."

Lydia held her lips tightly, determined not to cry.

"I'm sorry I did that. Tell me we're okay," Alan whispered.

Lydia nodded.

"Say it."

"I can't say that right now, Alan. I can't let you get away with hitting me. Jesus, I don't have arms or legs and you still think *hitting* me is okay?" She grew louder, each word angrier.

Alan retreated to the bed, his hands shaking. "It wasn't supposed to hurt."

"Oh, it didn't. Don't think you've *hurt* me, Alan. Don't even. You shouldn't have even dared slap me like that. You'll be making this up to me for a long time, buddy."

Alan stood and headed for the door.

"Where the hell are you going?" Lydia said, nearly shouting.

Alan twisted the knob and stood there, Lydia thinking he looked like a soap opera actor about to say something melodramatic.

He said, "I'm going to the airport, see what I can do about tickets."

"How many tickets?"

Alan held up two fingers.

"Good. We need to go somewhere warm. The cold hurts me."

Alan opened the door and stepped out, almost like he didn't hear. Lydia knew he heard every word. He would never hit her again. A momentary lapse, all the stress, she considered all that, but this slap was her power. It was the entire economy of their relationship until she was ready to let it drop. Maybe a few weeks. Maybe a couple months. Lydia took in a fine feeling breath and decided to play it by ear. Alan should lose more weight, maybe get a new nose, a new chin. He needed a demeanor of authority with others, submissive only to her, the perfect power couple. When Alan was ready, Lydia would let him know he was forgiven.

From her spot by the bathroom door, Megan heard their discussion. Two tickets, she assumed. Why else would the invalid bitch ask him about it? He was rattled about it, not sure of the next move until that woman laid it out like only she was able, no sugar with that medicine.

Two tickets. After a long gaze at Norm's soaked body, Megan knew who would be on that plane, wherever it was going.

Herself and Lancaster.

She eased off the wall and made a slow pirouette into the main room, a softly sinister expression painted on special for Lydia.

TWENTY-FIVE

Terry parked in a convenience store lot and waited. It was their third lot that hour. Lancaster must have been losing patience, but Terry was surprised at the guy's calmness. He explained the plan earlier, "Someone gets out, leave the thing running, we swoop in and at least get a few miles down the Interstate before we have to switch again. If we tried that in California, the police helicopters would find us. Not here."

Lancaster crossed his good arm over the cast, nodded, and said, "Let's do it."

Terry noticed that Lancaster had kept the older officer's badge, rubbing his thumb over the ridges.

They were on the side of the store, at the corner near the pay phone. Mostly invisible to the clerk inside except on the security monitor—one of the cameras was mounted near the self-serve island taking in the whole lot. As long as Terry pretended to use the phone a couple times, he was sure the clerk wouldn't think much. Lancaster's cast was a big thing, so he sat in the back, only ready to get out if Terry found a car.

The joint was lit up so bright that the evening blue-gray sky above the glow might as well have been midnight, only the neon casino signs along the beach breaking through. Terry mouthed a silent conversation into the phone propped between his ear and shoulder, hands balled in his pockets. It was funny how most times he stopped for gas, beer, or a *Hustler* at these places, some black kid or white gangsta wannabe pulled up in a tricked out Accord or Acura blaring skull-shaking rap bass, leaving the car running while he came in for a 64 oz. Mountain Dew to cool his buzz. Always the rap, never a country guy blaring Brooks and Dunn while getting more Skoal. As much as the rap guys bragged about their cars, Terry wondered why they almost *dared* someone to steal it by leaving it open and running for a song or two, almost a bullhorn announcement: "Hey, come and get it! Free car, you pussies!"

Thinking about that, Terry forgot to move his mouth, so he nodded, pretended to laugh. That's when someone pulled up in a pickup truck, nice little one, with a woman maybe in her forties driving. It was noisy, otherwise seemed in decent shape. The woman was floppy and had her hair pinned up, stretch shorts and a big T-shirt. She sat in her truck to finish a cigarette.

Terry hung up the phone, turned to the van, and nodded. He wasn't really sure how to do this since his mind needed rest and Lancaster had Terry double-guessing about things he normally took for granted. Why not trade the truck for the van? She would never go for it. It was at least a place to start.

He walked up to her and tapped on the glass. She didn't want to roll the window down. Terry put his palms together like prayer and mouthed *Please?*

She inched the window down.

"This is a one time deal, take it or leave it. I'll take this truck off your hands if you'll trade for that minivan," Terry said.

She laughed and shook her head. "This is a joke."

"Not a joke. It's a good van, good condition, not stolen or anything, you can check the glove box."

"That's just crazy."

"Look," Terry pointed back at the van. "It's only a year or two old compared to yours, which is maybe ten, it looks. You'll want to get rid of it soon anyway, so you get the best of both worlds. A van to drive in for a while, and better trade in value when you're ready to dump it."

The woman rolled the window up. Terry still heard her through the glass. "Please, get away from my truck. I need to buy a Pepsi, okay? I don't want your van."

Terry backed away from the truck, hands up to show he was cool with it. She watched him, shooed him back a couple of times until there was at least fifteen feet between them. She opened the door, holding it in case Terry was to lurch forward, he guessed. Then she stepped out.

Terry said, "Please, I know it's not normal, if you could take a minute to listen—"

"No, okay? Stop it already." She stalked into the store, careful to keep her eye on Terry until she was inside. The clerk must've been watching because the two started an instant conversation, both turning and gesturing at the parking lot, a few long glances.

He'll call the cops, Terry thought.

The clerk lifted the phone. Terry gnawed his lip and jittered, sharp breaths before he quick walked towards the van. Time to get on the road and try another method of getting a new ride.

That's when the van's side door slid back and Lancaster was out like he was flying, walking fast with the gun in his hand to the front door of the store. Terry froze in place and watched the horror show.

Lancaster pushed with his shoulder, slammed hard and shook the whole storefront—it was a pull only door. He shoved the gun in his sling, threw the door wide, then lifted the pistol and shot the clerk twice. Firecracker noise. He turned to the woman, who fell to the ground and wailed siren style. Three shots. The first shut her up, took it in the head, and Terry heard but couldn't watch the next shots. No need for so many bullets. No need for any of it.

He turned back to the store in time to see Lancaster stand up from a crouch, keys in hand. He kicked the door open and headed for the woman's truck. Terry started for it slowly, hoping passive resistance might end this sooner. *You don't want to get caught*, he thought.

"I also don't want to keep going," he mumbled as an answer.

Lancaster waited for Terry to come to the driver's door so he could hand over the keys. Terry took them.

"Your way sucked, you cunt."

"Jesus, I didn't think the point was to kill everyone in our way so we'll never get out of jail."

Lancaster smirked. "Where the hell else would you want to be? We'll be fucking legends, man."

Terry fell into the driver's seat without another word. Lancaster lingered too close for a moment too long. Terry pretended to adjust the rearview mirror until Lancaster stepped back with a loud sigh and slammed the door. Flinch, reflex, like a scary movie moment.

Lancaster made it to the passenger's side, tapped on the window, and Terry flicked the auto-unlock.

"We'll have to dump this one sooner than I thought," Terry said.

Lancaster sat down and closed the door, big grin stretching his skin all wrong. "Sounds fun."

He played with the radio while Terry backed out and started to weave up back streets on his way to the Interstate.

Fun.

Terry remembered the look on the girl's face as he held her down so

Lancaster could fuck her. The way this woman in the store convulsed when the gun blast hit her. Then he caught his reflection in the rearview. Puffy purple cheek. Jesus, Lancaster's idea of fun.

TWENTY-SIX

Alan stared at the arrivals and departures in the Delta terminal at Louis Armstrong International Airport. The Big Easy treated its jazz stars like royalty. Other than the name, though, it was a goddamn airport like other airports, crowded and everyone on edge except the business travelers who played at being bored. Still, Alan thought they were all staring at him, fish out of water, *big* fish out of his small pond. He wiped sweat from his face and crossed his arms, deciphering the numbers that flashed and changed before his eyes.

They were looking at him. The guard with the beer belly, the kids sitting with their mother on molded blue plastic chairs, the guy in the suit with the cell phone. The glass doors kept sliding open for people to enter and leave. Alan was convinced that every slide would bring the cops with handcuffs. Two pair linked together, the only way they'd fit. Hell, a couple months ago, even that might not have worked.

It didn't look like the Southwest was a good option that night. Instead, he was thinking about the flight to Miami. Go there, lay low, get some new ID, and then find a way out of the country with Lydia. He would find her another set of beautiful arms and legs, then buy her the finest silk dresses, the best wheelchair, a house overlooking the beach. Mexico was obvious. Alan was thinking about Costa Rica, Cuba, or to really stretch it, Fiji. Way off the map, no more crime or gambling or shady friends.

And when he made some money, he'd leave her.

The thought had been showing up more often the past few days. At first, he shook it off like it was Satan offering an apple, then it started to take root, all the alternative lives he could be living, the places he could go. Lydia gave him the confidence to be this new guy, so it was her own fault Alan wanted to flaunt it for other women, those he would never have dreamed of approaching before.

When the thought came recently—*leave her stumpy ass, go be James Bond or Magnum PI somewhere*—he let it sit there and grow before coming back to earth. Tough call, because it wasn't only sex or a crush. This was a serious relationship, and Alan could barely imagine life without her. Didn't really want to. He remembered all the shit he'd put up so far, feeling like she held his balls in one of those fake hands—except she could really squeeze. Little moments of life without that stress were looking not so bad.

Like that moment staring at the Delta departures.

Miami. A flight out at 9:35.

He thumbed through his wallet, hoping he had missed something so he wouldn't have to go up there and ask to buy two tickets, cash, no ID. *Yeah, sure. Not these days.*

It was hidden in the back because he only used it once, after losing some weight on the Atkins diet Lydia told him to try. A fake ID, Ronnie's driver's license with Alan's photo on it. He did it to use a Discover card Ronnie had left at Lydia's place. She gave it to him, told him to get some new clothes for his new body.

Alan glanced down at himself, the gut still flabby though much smaller, the khakis snug instead of monstrous. Sweat stains under the arms more from nerves than body heat.

The Discover card was paid down, something Lydia handled, so maybe that would work. It was the last thing to try. He thought driving was still a better idea. Lydia was signing their confession wanting to fly. *Fuck it.*

If he got caught, he would spill on Lydia so fast, cut a deal, get himself in good with the prosecutors, all the work he had done for so many Gulf Coast wiseguys bound to pay off at last. Like someone told him once: *Hope for the best, expect the worst.*

He stalked toward a Delta desk, hoping for Miami, expecting jail.

Megan strolled over to Lydia, one foot carefully in front of the other like a debutante, fingers laced behind her back, little schoolgirl smirk. Lydia's stare was powerless. Her quick breathing gave her away. Damn it, that wasn't the way to control things. Lydia was truly fucking scared of this girl.

It was her first time to really take in little Megan, scrawny bird legs with scarred knees and shins, sort of neo-punkish beauty the kids went for, all retro Seventies except for girly barrettes and goth hair dye. The blonde looked real enough, pink residue on the tips, Lydia noticed. The girl's eyes were dead. Lydia could do the dead-eye look, but Megan's was a natural thing. What the hell was she doing here? It showcased a flaw in Alan's programming—not killing her on the road and dumping her body in the woods. He wasn't that tough yet. Maybe he would never be.

Megan's tiny steps closed in on Lydia, the girl's blouse brushing Lydia's shoulder. She rolled her head to the other side, the only move she had in the arsenal. If not tied to the chair, maybe she had a lurch or two left in her. She should have asked Alan to untie her, lay her on the bed. Visions of prison nightmares sparked in her head.

Megan stroked her fingers through Lydia's hair.

"Don't touch me."

"No one's paid attention to your hair. It needs brushing," Megan said.

"It's fine."

Megan went to the overnight kit on the dresser, opened it and fumbled through. She pulled out a brush and stepped back Lydia's chair, stood behind her and brushed. She caught a tangle, yanked, tried again.

"Not so hard."

"Oh, I'm sorry," Megan said.

So fake.

"It's hard to tell, you know. I'll be careful. Speak up if I'm rough." Megan eased the brush into Lydia's hair and was much more gentle, holding the tangles in her free hand to avoid hurting her. The bristles felt a little rough on her scalp, but it wasn't so bad. Lydia even closed her eyes a moment, remembering how Alan loved to do this almost every night. She almost asked Norm that one night he fed her peaches, then decided to keep that between her and Alan—one of those special small things.

Megan did a nice gentle job. Lydia had never been with a woman sexually, imagined if it was this soft—the feeling of brush and thin fingers on her scalp, the girl's perfume clean in the air. Lydia's mind wandered and she saw herself, long arms and legs, with this naked skinny nurse on top of her, kissing her breasts, the warmth between them comfortable like a long bath.

Megan said in a low voice, "He can't always be around. You need someone like me along."

"I know," Lydia said, the spell then broken. Fucking little manipulator. *If only she would've kept her mouth shut.* Everything with these kids was melodramatic, music video obvious. "I need a good nurse and a friend."

"I'm not a nurse, you know."

"Hm?"

"I can learn what to do, I guess."

What was the uniform all about? What the hell was her game? Lydia thought. Funny how people assume so much on looks alone. Funny how no one thought she was anything but a curious nurse. Even funnier she would confess it now, unless the girl really wanted to be accepted.

"How's Norm?" Lydia said.

"Norm?"

"I thought I heard you talking to him. Why were you running the water?"

"I don't know. Poor guy."

Lydia knew he had been hurt, didn't know how bad it was. Alan said something about not having to kill him if things kept going the way they were. Must've been terrible. "You like Norm, then?"

"He was sweet. Ugly, but sweet. I don't know. Not really my type. I could've seen being interested if he looked better."

"He looked better when he was younger."

"Maybe he kept up with the styles a little more back then."

Lydia noticed she talked about him in past tense, wondered if it meant something or if the girl didn't see a difference—past, present, future, same shit, different day.

The brush sliced through, followed by Megan's fingertips, such a delicate touch. Lydia was lulled again, eyes closing involuntarily, thoughts again drifting to Megan's affections.

"You think Alan'll leave you?" Megan said.

"Why?"

"Do you think he'll be desperate for, I guess, like, a *touch* or something? Would you let him have someone else occasionally to satisfy that if you knew he still loved you?"

The image in Lydia's mind, the naked Megan, was the one speaking. Lydia felt powerless to this little angel, fingers gentle and knowing.

"You mean *you*?" Lydia said.

"No, not me, I wouldn't do that. Anyone else?"

"We don't even think like that. It's real love, sacrificial love. I've never felt it this way before."

The brush slowed.

"Megan?"

"Hm?"

"What if I said I wanted it to be you? Because I know you don't love him. For me, would you do that?"

The girl giggled a little. In Lydia's mind vision, Megan rolled her head on her shoulders, lifted her arms and stretched, arched her back, Lydia loving every curve, every pale inch of the girl's body.

"What if it were all three of us?" Megan said.

A mind reader, Lydia thought. *Where was the harm? It was only talk.*

"All three. Tell me more."

"Candles. I would light so many candles, and I would undress you while he watched. And then—*Jesus Christ!*" Megan's voice caught.

Lydia opened her eyes and snorted a sharp breath. A sad imitation of Norm stood in the bathroom doorway. He could barely hold himself up, leaning heavy on the jamb. He was soaked head to toe, white like death, and one of his hands was wrapped in a thick towel, cradled on his stomach.

The fog lifted and Norm let out his breath. The water drained slowly until there was a sucking sound at the drain, so close it brought him fully back. He blinked and huffed heavily until he could see without clouds, double vision. His hand was only there in pain, no other feeling, not able to flex. It felt asleep and on fire at the same time. He was cold, sticky. He grabbed the faucet with his good hand and pulled until he could inch over and sit on the edge of the tub. That was all right. His legs felt strong enough. He lifted one leg over the tub to the tile floor. A towel was bunched down there. He lifted it, wrapped it around his mangled hand.

Then the voices from the other room, light and sweet. Megan and Lydia. Norm stood. A little nauseous, not enough to heave. He made small steps to the door, leaned on it, and saw Megan brushing Lydia's hair, both women with satisfied expressions, the world at peace for a change. Then Megan saw him, strangled out a few words. Lydia opened her eyes. He wondered if this was pity, fear, hate, a mix.

Whatever it was, it gave Norm the strength to believe he would live. A useless hand, and a new start from scratch. With these two women in his life, he knew he would be okay.

Megan started towards him. "What is it? How are you doing?"

Norm cleared his throat and whispered, "Can I get out of these clothes and climb in the bed?"

Megan grinned enough to make him happy. She rubbed his shoulder and said, "Welcome back."

TWENTY-SEVEN

Two cars later, Terry drove a black Camry into the rest area a few miles past the Louisiana state line. He parked, got out and stretched. Lancaster was out of the car heading for the bathroom in record time. So he had to piss, okay, though after the horror show of a day he'd been through, Terry didn't want to take any chances. He followed, Lancaster already out of sight by the time Terry made it up the sloping path curving to the side of the building, the restroom entrance.

Inside, Lancaster was leaning over a urinal, cast resting on the porcelain top, while another man, bulky in an Ozzfest T-shirt, washed his hands and inspected his beard. A third guy stood at the urinal farthest from the door. If there was going to be trouble, it would be with this guy, maybe in his fifties and dressed in tan slacks and a designer sports shirt. Rimless glasses, cell phone clipped to his belt. He probably carried a money clip and a few high-limit credit cards.

Terry turned into the nearest stall and closed the door, hoping Lancaster had missed him. He tried to take a piss. Nothing came. Dry, dry, dry. He hopped in place, trying to bounce out a nervous stream. Only a few drops sputtered. He zipped up, stepped away, and the automatic flush kicked in. Terry ducked his head low to see if anyone else was in a stall, felt misty flush drops on his cheek. The other stalls were empty. The parking lot had been mostly empty, and daylight was finally gone except for a dark dim gray that only helped gauge where the treeline stopped. He thought about the cars in the lot, the Audi sedan probably belonging to this fancy guy in the restroom. *Any family waiting? Kids and wife? Maybe inside the main building or in the other restroom. Lancaster won't care.*

Before, this situation would have been handled with a little patience. Terry needed to get a lay of the land before deciding how much muscle was needed. Most times, a subtle hint was enough, and they could've left with the fancy guy's car, money, phone, without feeling rushed. The *story* was the thing, not the threat. People listened, believed.

Starting with that trooper, when the story was falling to pieces and Lancaster shot him instead of letting Terry find a new angle, everything began to change. He could tell that Lancaster was itchy at the pool guy's house, holding it in. After getting shot, though, Lancaster acted on impulse, much like he did when he and Terry first teamed up, back when he was a simple convenience store robber barely making a living. Terry changed that, gave them a steady income, extra cash, relative safety. The last several hours had seen them tally up more felonies and dead bodies than during the entire partnership, going on six years. Terry had never been more afraid.

One urinal flushed. The other right behind it. Terry heard a scuffle, an apology, then a *Hey!* quickly muffled. He peeked out of his stall to see Lancaster holding the guy against the wall, cast pressed against his throat and free hand over his mouth.

Lancaster turned his head and said, "Keys!"

Yeah, he had seen Terry try to sneak in. Should've known better. He played brawn but had a bright criminal's brain lurking under the impulsiveness. Terry stuck his head out, looked left and right. The bearded guy was gone. *No one else around. How much longer?*

"We don't need it," Terry said. "We're fine until we get there."

"I *like* it. Leather seats. I like that. What the fuck does it matter?"

Terry stepped over, getting a whiff of a clogged urinal along with Lancaster's slick unwashed body, musty. He felt the fancy guy's pockets, not knowing why he felt that way about this man, wearing the same things Terry liked to wear most days—Polo and Tommy and A&F, and nice brown Dexter boat shoes. There he was, ten notches down on the class scale, rifling through the guy's pockets like a fourteen-year-old gang member.

He found the keys, the money clip he knew would be there, the phone, and the wallet. The fancy man's face crawled beneath Lancaster's palm, wanting to plead for his life, wanting to relate to these men somehow. Probably worried about getting sliced, getting raped. Poor son of a bitch had no idea. It would be quicker than that, God only knew how painless.

"That all?" Lancaster said.

Terry nodded. Lancaster didn't say anything, so Terry spoke up. "I've got it all."

"Shoes," Lancaster said.

"What?"

"Check his shoe size."

Terry knelt, half-expecting a knee to the face from one of them. He slipped the guy's shoe off, maroon sock held up trying to avoid touching the floor. Terry found the tag.

"Eleven."

"Yeah, okay. Maybe. Put it down."

Terry placed it beside Lancaster's foot. His partner slipped off his flip-flop and stuck his foot in, struggled a little. Terry helped snug it over Lancaster's bare heel.

"Not bad. It'll do," Lancaster said. Then he pulled his cast away, grabbed the guy's shirt, and slammed him backward against the wall, his head smacking, echoing, bouncing. Lancaster pulled him forward, built momentum, and bashed the guy's forehead against the edge of a urinal pipe. It went red and dripped on the porcelain, and the fancy guy spasmed before going still. Lancaster worked off the other shoe while Terry checked for a pulse.

"Still alive, barely."

"Maybe he'll live, maybe not."

"We don't know if he's got family out there or what."

Lancaster's grin turned Terry's stomach. "You want to go look? Easy enough to find out."

"Let's just go, all right? I'm happy enough you didn't kill him."

"Adds to the variety of charges, you know?" Lancaster leaned on the wall while trying to push is way into the other shoe, finally giving up, walking on the heel as he passed Terry. "It's one thing to kill. Now this guy might be a vegetable, a retard or something. Worse than dying, if you ask me."

Terry followed him out of the restroom, looking around for signs that someone heard, or maybe a wife or girlfriend waiting. Nothing. Lancaster walked gimpy on the heel of the boat shoe, saying he would fix it in the car. As they reached the Audi, beautiful piece of work, black A4, another vehicle's lights pulled in from the interstate. Then another right behind. Terry and Lancaster hopped into the car before anyone got a good look, pulled out of the parking spot, then eased the Audi back to the road.

The car was a 5-speed, fine interior, bad-ass engine. The type of car *anyone* would notice coming into a rest area. Terry loved this machine, but wished for the Camry instead, paranoia pretty much taking over whatever control confidence used to play in his thinking.

"Any more stops?" Terry said.

Lancaster clucked his tongue, rolled his head around before reclining the seat. "Not until the hotel. I'll give her a call when we get closer."

"How are you going to call her? They check in under her real name?"

Lancaster rolled his head Terry's direction, lazy glance. "I've got magic, you know. Big magic. I see all."

Then he laughed and slapped Terry's shoulder, said, "She told me her room number, dumbass."

Terry waited a long time before saying, "Those people will find the guy back there. They'll remember this car."

"Then you'd better get busy looking innocent."

TWENTY-EIGHT

When he came back from the airport, Alan was surprised to see a couple of things—Norm alive and asleep in one of the beds, and Lydia looking gorgeous again, hair brushed and untangled, face washed. Megan had been busy. Or it was Lydia reasserting herself, playing with the little girl's mind like it was putty, shaping her to help get back at Alan for that slap.

Lydia's face held a peaceful expression tightly, as if moving it would cause it to crack like dry clay. Her eyes told him nothing. Megan sat on the edge of the empty bed on the side nearest Norm. Her arms were over-straight, elbows pointing inward, the bones sharp at the angle. She rocked back and forth.

Alan waggled a couple of fingers at Norm. "What the hell's this? You take pity on him?"

Megan stood. "He got out on his own. What were we supposed to do?"

"I don't know. Fuck, he can't be okay."

"He might make it."

Alan said, "A couple hours ago, you wanted to drown him. Now you're his guardian angel?"

She stepped closer. "All right, then what can we do? You seem to be in charge, I guess, so tell us how we should handle poor pathetic Norm."

Alan wanted to backhand her across the room, chase her down, beat her until the tears were real, the bruises dark, smart-ass bitch. She deserved it. She deserved it so much. She did. He couldn't touch her.

Instead, he twisted his hips, shouted to Lydia, "Sweetie?"

Lydia's eyes narrowed, her face ticking as she bored an imaginary hole through Megan. "We don't have a choice anymore."

"We can leave him asleep, can't we?"

"And if they find him before our plane lands?"

Alan nodded, then grabbed a pillow off the empty bed and straddled Norm, pressed the pillow over his face with all the force and pressure he could. His muscles tensed, breathing strained, holding on against the thrashing man beneath him, the shrieks of little Megan trying to pull him off. Her hands felt like a light breeze and had no effect at all as he pressed the pillow down, down, harder, down, hold on.

Norm kicked, not able to buck Alan off. Norm thrashed and hit, didn't have the power. His head pivoted left right left right left—

Then weaker.

Then weaker still.

Nothing at all.

Alan kept the pressure up. It wasn't heat of the moment anymore, or displaced anger at Megan, or a reflex caused by fear. For once, he made a real choice to kill—Norm was a problem. Alan had two tickets for Miami leaving in about two hours, and he was going to be on that flight with one of these women, preferably Lydia, and that meant getting rid of two inconvenient leeches. Better now when the redneck fuck was defenseless than when he was awake and energized.

The difference between "dead" and "passed out" was maybe three more minutes. Alan kept the pressure up, the girl now beating, scraping with her nails, yanking his hair, kicking. And when his arms threatened to give out, he yanked the pillow away.

Norm stared up at him with startled wide eyes, bulging and blood-shot, his lips parted, his pale skin mottled. No breath.

Alan felt sick, turned his head to the room behind him. Megan had sunk to her knees, crying in heaves, barely able to breathe. *She didn't care about him*, Alan thought. *She's crying because she's next.*

He dismounted, stood between the beds, inches from Megan. Something burned on his neck. He pressed fingertips back there—stung—and looked at them. Blood. She had scratched him good. Then he grinned.

"Sweetie?" Lydia said.

"Yes, babe?"

Lydia was quiet a long time, emotionless, pale. Then, "Where are we going?"

Alan pulled the tickets from his back pocket and held them up. "Miami. It's a good place to start getting lost before we go somewhere else."

Lydia's face lit up the way a Princess' might if she were told the Queen was dead. "Come here."

Alan stepped over Megan, who was now quiet, listening as her fate was decided. He eased towards Lydia, knelt in front of her chair.

"My leg is itching, Alan. Do like you used to. Please, it's itching so bad."

Like a veteran mime, he smoothed his palms over the phantom leg, the shape of the prosthetic burned in his memory as he imagined it there in front of him, knowing Lydia saw it too, as sure as there was nothing there, it was there. Her warm living leg. Alan started with the foot, eased up her calf.

"Tell me where. Here?" he said.

"Higher than that. It's hard to pinpoint."

His hands rounded the knee, slowed as he went along her thigh. "Closer?"

"God, baby, you're right there. On the inside. Yes, that's almost, almost, so—you've got it, don't move."

His fingers scratched lightly in circles. His other hand rubbed the outside of her thigh. Something he was coming to understand, mind over matter, because for a moment, seeing the way Lydia believed her legs were there, her hands there probably ruffling his hair, Alan thought he really felt flesh. It was nice, reminded him of childhood days in church, the women in their knee-length dresses wearing white pantyhose, turning already beautiful legs into sculpture, masterpieces. *Didn't they know how sexy this was, and they dared come to church like this?* An affront to holiness.

When they first picked her up, Megan was wearing white stockings.

Lydia's head was bowed like prayer, eyes closed. She usually didn't close her eyes, because to keep the illusion, she had to watch.

Alan thought about white stockings. Megan wore hers on real legs. Skinny, scarred, but goddamnit, *real*.

His fingers stopped scratching. Lydia's eyes popped open.

She said, "What are you thinking?"

"Tomorrow. Just about tomorrow. We can look around, you know. Replace the prosthetics."

She looked confused. "What do you mean?"

"The ones we lost."

"Everything's where it should be, see?" Lydia said, and her expression was one of a woman pointing her toes, admiring her long arms. "See?"

He played along for the moment. Tonight was tonight and tomorrow would be tomorrow. New rules, new game.

"I'm sorry," he said. "I was thinking of someone else."

Her smile returned. "Those tickets. I did see *two*, right? You know all along it would only be two. You and me against the world."

Alan nodded, couldn't help grinning.

The phone rang and all the fantasies popped like balloons. Lydia and Alan turned to the phone on the nightstand between the beds.

Megan lunged for it, answered, "Hello?"

Alan didn't get up and bat it out of her hands or grab her or muzzle her lips with his huge hand, those choices running through his mind simultaneously. Instead, he held his breath.

Megan listened a moment, then spoke like answering an interview. "Yes. Yeah, that's it. Sure. The same, I told you already. Oh no, no, nothing, I didn't mean it. Yeah, me too."

She hung up, then stood. Face bright and puffy from crying, no more tears, no more little girl theatrics or outbursts. She was calm, cool, and in control.

Alan turned to Lydia, her lips trembling mad. He said, "We've got to get out of here."

TWENTY-NINE

Lancaster flipped the cell phone shut and pointed off to the right. "You can see the sign from here. Turn in, find the car, find one sixty-two, and I guess we win."

"You don't think they'll fight back?"

"Sure, Crabtree will. I'll gut shoot him. The gimp woman is a fucking doorstop, man. I was thinking, if you want, you can fuck her before we kill her. I want her to die slow, helplessly, like leaving her upside down on the toilet or something."

Terry said, "Jesus," and turned his attention to the planes taking off from the dark field, the rumble and the lights, a smaller jet landing on the opposite side.

"I said *right*, asshole. You're going to pass it."

Terry looked right and saw the motel, pulled hard right and bounced into the parking lot.

"Go around the side," Lancaster said, leaning forward in his seat, face inches from the windshield. He mumbled a little mantra, "One six two, one six two, one six two, *shit!*"

Terry rounded the side of the main building in time to see Alan Crabtree leaning into the passenger side of his car, belting the limbless woman in her seat. Megan stood on the sidewalk with her arms crossed, behind her the room door wide open. Crabtree looked up, then backed away, slammed the door, and rushed around to the other side. His girth got in the way and he bounced off the fender and the hood ornament as he jogged to the driver's door.

"Ram him, goddamnit!" Lancaster said. He was frantic, shaking his gun, having to lay it down while he lowered the window.

"I'm not ramming the guy, come on."

"Block him in, or something."

"You're not going to shoot him in the parking lot, are you? We wouldn't make it five blocks."

Lancaster turned to Terry, lifted the gun and bapped him on the shoulder with it. Terry flinched left and hit the brakes, the car stuttering. Burning, torn skin, he wanted to cry. He threw the car into park and flung the door wide open before Lancaster could say anything.

"He can get around," Lancaster shouted.

Terry stood outside the car, hands on his hips, taking a deep trance look at everything in front of him. Megan ran for their car, saying something he couldn't understand. Crabtree backed out of the spot too fast, barely in control as he shot forward and missed the other car only by swerving.

Lancaster opened the door but closed it again as Crabtree drove past, then Lancaster was out of the car with a gun aimed, cheeks puffed out wide. He went from *sure-shot* to *maybe* to *lost the chance* within five seconds. Megan ran to Lancaster's side, her words lost in jet backwash until the last few seconds.

"—the airport in two hours."

Lancaster stared at the road. "Where they going?"

"Miami, at first. If you want him, you have to get him before they get there. They plan on getting lost."

"Get to Miami or the airport?"

"Pretty much the same thing now, right?"

They seemed at ease with each other talking like that, but they didn't hug or kiss, Terry noticed. They had something else, like they knew to hold the affection for later. They had the same *mind* about things, the same intensity. This little alternachick understood the new Lancaster better than Terry did.

"So," Megan said, "We get the hell out of here because they left a dead guy in the room and we don't want anyone to get a good look at us."

"Who's dead?" Terry said.

"Norm, the little guy at the hospital? I thought I had killed him but then he was alive and I thought it was, like, a sign." She patted Lancaster's shoulder. "See? He came back to tell me I was okay. Then that fat asshole smothered him."

Lancaster nodded, then yelled *"Fuck"* and stomped the ground in his new boat shoes. A dark expression over the roof of the car, aimed at Terry. Then, Lancaster shot around so fast before Terry could take off running. Lancaster grabbed him, shook hard. Terry lost his footing and went down, Lancaster's fingers still twisting his shirt front, the collar rubbing Terry's neck raw like fire, and Lancaster pulling him inches away from that awful face, wrinkled and twisted and sunken.

"I'm going to hurt you," Lancaster said, dead flat calm. "I'm going to hurt you in a way that will make you *never* question me again, or treat me like I'm a mindless thug who works for you instead of us being equal partners."

"Please, man, I never—"

"I mean it will hurt and it won't stop for a long time. I might make you my bitch, literally, and then keep at you like I'm waiting for you to spill troop movements and secret codes."

"Time to move," Megan said loudly. She hopped in the backseat of the Audi.

Lancaster let go of Terry's shirt and backed away, still staring at him without blinking. "That wasn't idle threat, bro. It's going to hurt worse than anything ever, and I promise, if we still haven't been caught after taking out Crabtree, your ass is mine. Now drive us to the airport."

Terry walked to the car on reflex, his mind painting big pictures—arrows and *Exit* and *This Way Out* and more arrows flashing like neon pointing in every direction except towards that Audi. Still, he dropped into the driver's seat as Lancaster eased into the other side. Megan moved forward, wrapped her arms around Lancaster's shoulders. Terry glanced in the rearview at Megan's face snuggling the back of Lancaster's head with an impish grin like a *manga* character.

"Let's roll, partner," Lancaster said, his good hand covering Megan's little fingers on his chest.

Terry didn't know which one of them Lancaster was speaking to. *Not me*, he thought. *Not for much longer.*

THIRTY

It was a silent ride. It probably shouldn't have been. Alan needed a plan, and Lydia didn't have one ready. Go straight to the airport? They would be sitting ducks. Drive around the area for another hour? Even if they did, what if Terry and Lancaster went straight to the airport and waited?

This part of town was crowded with chain restaurants, motels, small businesses falling apart from the signs to the paint jobs to the bad parking lots, lot of troublemaking kids out wandering the streets trying to look like gang members even though the kids were scared of the real thing if they were to see them. It wasn't touristy New Orleans, the sprawling underclass suburbs, sinking into the Gulf of Mexico at the same rate as the rest of the city.

Alan stopped at a red light and kept checking his rearview. He was sweating again and having chills. He cleared his throat constantly, kept his eyes ahead, not risking a glance at Lydia's disappointed frown. He'd seen enough of that to last a lifetime.

Finally she said, "Once we get there and get through security, they won't let anyone in the terminal without a boarding pass. We've still got a head start."

Alan nodded.

"No luggage to check," she said.

"We tell them it's an emergency, last minute trip, and we'll buy some overnight stuff at the airport."

"That's a good idea. Okay. Sweetie, we're going to be fine, so breathe easy, calm down."

"The little bitch was working with him the whole time. She wanted us dead. And we let it happen."

Lydia's voice was calm when she said, "You're the one who didn't kill her in the ambulance and cut her to pieces. You were the one who let her keep tagging along. There's not much I can do unless you listen to me."

"I'm sorry."

"She wanted to survive and get what was best for her, same as us. Right at the end there, if they hadn't found us, you were finally ready to kill her."

Alan blinked. "Yeah."

The light turned green, and Alan had to figure a way to get in the right lane to turn around and make for the airport. The traffic was thick and slow, his blinker not making any difference as he dripped along at ten miles an hour, cars behind him honking, while the cars in the right lane passed and passed. Finally, he revved the motor and stuck himself in front of a Cherokee that was coming up quickly. It flashed hi-beams, honked a long blast. Alan pulled in front, ignored the light show, and turned into the parking lot of a shopping center. He could cut across it to the side road that led to the airport entrance.

The Cherokee pulled in behind him, lights still flashing.

"This is bullshit," he said.

"Ignore him and he'll get tired. Stop and we lose time."

Alan wove through the half-empty lot, home of a K-mart that had seen better days, and a few small stores with hand-painted signs—*A Cut Above Salon, Jim's Cards and Comics, China Buffet*. The Cherokee stayed right behind, almost tapping the bumper of the Monte Carlo.

"Fucking moron—"

Lydia said, "Let it go."

"If he touches the car—"

"It's not like you're ever going to see it again after we park it, right?"

A van pulled out of a parking lot suddenly, one of the reverse lights out, and Alan slammed on brakes. The Cherokee was too close, bumped the Monte Carlo hard. The hard plastic light covers shattered.

Alan threw the car into park before Lydia could say anything. He was out of the car as his name left her lips.

The Cherokee driver was out, too. Just a guy with a slight gut, half-bald, in a denim shirt. He was ready to be mad, ready to threaten lawsuits and talk without stopping for breath. He was yammering the second Alan started towards him.

"So, you think it's my fault now? No, I've got a case here and witnesses, pal. You cut me off, no signal, then you slam on your brakes out of spite. Don't even try to argue, because there's no way this would've happened had it not been for you. That's the law."

Alan checked the Cherokee. No other passengers. A bucket of chicken on the floorboard, tipped over. Same with mashed potatoes, a drink in the cup holder angled out, lid popped off.

Alan grabbed the guy by the throat. He was all for strangling tonight. Seemed easy. Seemed the quickest way out of this. In the back of his mind, a little replay of his murders ran with a meter underneath measuring how afraid he was each time. Remorseful, too. Shooting Cap, off the meter, wild red zone panic. Killing Tompkins, a spike to the middle but then calm, only to spike up again when Terry and Lancaster showed up. Almost killing Lancaster, the needle dropped to almost dead nothing. Smothering Norm, sure, a small spike there, more adrenaline than fear, though.

This Cherokee driver. Not registering anything. He was in the way.

Alan's fingers clamped into this guy's throat, pinching the arteries, and Alan's body pinned the man against the driver's seat, arms and legs immobile. Alan looked around, saw no witnesses. If they were in cars, he couldn't tell, and if there were a security camera scanning the lot, then fuck it, he was screwed anyway.

You want to keep living like this? Kill anyone who gets in your way because of her?

Only a few days before, Alan was close to calling that gaming school, see if he could teach. A snapshot of him back behind the board, four students watching his every move and taking notes. No fear, no danger. No Lydia, though. He desperately wanted her in his life, but without the drama, the money, or the power, she would grow bored.

The man went limp. Alan let go. He almost shouted to Lydia, *Pop the trunk*, before remembering he had to do it himself. He propped the driver against the tire and ran to the Monte Carlo, reached over Lydia and pressed the trunk release in the glove compartment. He didn't look at her.

At the Cherokee again, he lifted the driver to his feet and moved him to the trunk, let him drop inside. He banged the man's head going down, then again inside on the jack. He was twisted sideways. Alan lifted the rubbery legs and tucked them inside, slammed the trunk. Tight fit. The back bumper was scratched, dented deep, and the taillight cover was in shards on the ground, the bulb busted, too. Perfect excuse for a cop to pull them over, but moving Lydia to the Cherokee would take too long.

One more scan for witnesses, security cameras. His paranoia kicked in—*on the road, people with cell phones could've seen. All those people passing by.* Fuck them all. Keep moving. The tickets, the plane, before anyone figures anything out, he and Lydia would be in the air.

Alan parked the Cherokee in an empty slot, then climbed into the Monte Carlo again, buckled up, and drove off the way he had wanted to go in the first place.

Quiet in the car except for Alan's heavy breathing. He caught himself, eased air through his nose, calmly, easily, peacefully, numbingly.

Lydia said, "I'm not mad. You don't have to worry about me being mad. I think he would've given up following us after a couple of miles. And now we've lost some time. I'm not mad. Maybe worried."

"Stop worrying."

"If they beat us there by even a little."

"They get within ten feet, I'm yelling like a baby. Security will shoot him down before anything happens."

"What if they wait in the parking garage? What if they wait on the shoulder of the road before we even get on the ramp?" Lydia said.

Alan's confidence crumbled, hearing Lydia scared like that. She was always rock steady and sure of a way out. So, was this a trap? Waltzing into the airport if Lancaster was already there, hiding, ready to pounce, no win situation. Same if they made it on the plane and the cops got it all figured out before they landed, waiting in Miami to take them off the plane. Or if they drove, broken taillight, tried to make it somewhere safe with a two-state manhunt full-bore. No one escaped anymore. *America's Most Wanted* took care of that.

"Please, we can't do this," he said.

"Can't what?"

"No changing now. We've got tickets. Let's just go use the tickets."

THIRTY-ONE

Megan told Lancaster about the ambulance ride, about Lydia and Crabtree, about the shoot out with the cops, about Norm's resurrection and how Crabtree killed him again. She told these things to Lancaster softly, close to his ear. Terry listened, caught most of the conversation, though it was clear that she wasn't talking to him, only to Lancaster. Terry's role was defined back at the motel—a bitch slap, a good threat, and he was a lowly driver. Lancaster's punk.

"Their flight leaves at nine-thirty," Megan said.

"I know, you said that."

"What do you want to do?"

Lancaster took a deep breath and stared out his window. They followed signs as best they could to get to the airport. Terry didn't know any shortcuts. He stayed right, slow, careful. He finally found a sign that made things more clear, turned right at a light and found himself in lanes with signs above pointing to terminals, long-term parking, arrivals, departures. Thick traffic.

"We should park in the garage, get a different car on the way out," Terry said.

"There won't be a way out."

"Sure there will."

Lancaster smiled. Terry even thought Megan looked a bit surprised by that.

"We do what we need to do, and we leave. We always leave," Terry said, then wishing he hadn't because it sounded condescending.

Megan nuzzled Lancaster's neck, her fingertips roaming. "Baby?"

Lancaster grunted, sat straight, moved Megan's hand, then turned to both of them.

"We can't get guns in there. We probably can't get knives. We should be happy they stopped searching cars finally. This thing we've got to do, we improvise. Steal a guard's gun or strangle Crabtree with a shoestring, whatever. And with all these people, how do we get out without a fucking shootout or chase?" Lancaster's eyes flicked back and forth between Megan and Terry. "I'm not going to surrender. This is it, what it all leads up to."

Terry shook his head. "And I'm supposed to go down with you, no questions asked?"

Lancaster's smile went Cheshire Cat. "Partners, bro."

Megan didn't come this far to commit suicide, especially after having a second shot at innocence. Seeing Norm alive was like being born again.

She felt so close to Lancaster, though, like this was her soulmate, so the blaze of glory stuff surprised the hell out of her. She sat in the middle of the backseat as they climbed the ramps into the upper sections of the parking garage, thinking maybe Lancaster's play was a bluff, a cry for attention. What she would do was change his mind. Yeah, show him all he has to live for with her in the picture. The places they would go, the people they would hurt, the drugs they would share.

Maybe there was sex, too, but not the primary thing. She had sex anytime she wanted, with friends and one night stands and older men who wanted to possess her, friends of her dad, even. Megan knew sex, knew what she liked, understood her body and its responses better than most women knew their own. What she missed, except for a relationship a few years before that lasted a year and a half, was intimacy. Not *Lifetime* TV or women's magazine bullshit intimacy, either. She was talking spiritual refreshment, psychic renewal.

Yes, there would be sex with Lancaster, she was certain. The more exciting part was this instant intimacy she experienced so wholly in those first moments and the brief conversations, and now in the same car with him. He was also a wild card, unpredictable, exactly what she wanted—a life of surprise, the death of boredom, of her old self.

Terry pulled the car into a tight spot between a Suburban and a pickup. He was pretty tense, more sunken and pale than Megan remembered him being at the hospital. Her impression, pretty fresh, was that Terry had been reduced to a tag-along. If *he* were left holding the bag at the end of this, then she could get Lancaster all to herself.

Opening the doors and getting out proved to be a tight squeeze. She and Lancaster exited on the same side while Terry stayed behind to wipe prints off as best he could, do a final search for loose hair, threads, blood spots. They lingered at the trunk as Terry combed the floorboard. Megan leaned into Lancaster, and he wrapped his good arm around her.

"Just promise me you'll try to live," she said.

"What do you mean?"

"Let's say things go better than you think they will in here—"

"They won't."

"No, hold on, let's say they do. I want you to try to make it out okay. For me?"

"Shit, I thought you'd be down with it."

"I'm down with it later, sure. Bonnie and Clyde, hip hip hooray. For now, like, we can have some fun. I've been dreaming of it."

Lancaster's face softened a little, his lips grinning and fighting it. He squeezed her closer. She wished they could abandon the whole plan and leave.

"Let him take the fall," Megan blurted, not even aware for a moment that she said it, a pouty whine.

Lancaster said, "I've been thinking about that."

Megan lifted her head. "Really?"

"I don't know, maybe. We've been together a long time, and I owe him for getting me out of the hospital. Stuff's different now. Still, you know, friends are friends."

"You don't treat him like a friend, what I saw."

Lancaster shrugged. "Like any other relationship. Good and bad, up and down. Used to be he would talk people out of money. I was a backup plan, sometimes just stood by looking mean. If we got in trouble, same thing. Let him ease us out of there. And it was a fifty-fifty deal, not like either of us was any more important, right? It worked."

"So what happened?"

She felt the sigh leave his chest, long and tough.

He said, "I got tired of waiting for him. Life's too short."

Megan slid against him, tiptoes, lips giving him a sweet smack on the cheek. "That's what I'm telling you. You don't have to wait on me. I'm right with you, spur of the moment. And the other thing is, relationships end sometimes. They just do. Fighting to keep them makes it worse, and makes you fight with the one you want to keep. So, why not try a different partner for awhile?"

The car door slammed behind them. Terry ambled out, hands deep in his pockets. He looked ashamed, Megan thought. It wasn't exactly fear. More like he thought everyone was laughing at him for pissing his pants.

"All done," he said quietly.

"Let's move, then."

Lancaster waited for Terry to take the lead, then he walked by Megan's side, his arm on her shoulder and hers on his back.

He whispered to her, "You've got a point. Something to think about."

THIRTY-TWO

The scary part was being alone. Surrounded by thousands, Lydia was alone. Alan had pulled up to the Delta departures curb, jumped out and explained the situation to the first person in a Delta uniform he saw. Lydia watched from her seat, hoping they wouldn't check the trunk, wishing it was easier. The story was simple—*family emergency, last moments of Mom's life, so we had to leave in a hurry and catch any plane we could. Didn't even have time to bring Lydia's big electric wheelchair.*

Alan talked a few minutes, then got some nods, and the Delta employee disappeared inside the terminal. Alan turned to the car, grinned weakly, showed her a thumbs up. The employee returned a minute later with a wheelchair, and she walked out to the car with Alan. The employee was a severe-looking woman, Mediterranean, the dark skin and eyes, with dark hair pulled back tightly. Her thin lipped pleasantness was false, for the sake of her job. Lydia still burned over Megan's double-cross. Not that she had done it, because Lydia knew she would, but that she had hidden it so well.

The self-obsessed little whore wasn't perfect. She needed others to make anything work at all, the way she hitched the ride with Alan. The way she needed Lancaster to save her at the last second. Yeah, her weakness—alone, she was useless.

Same as you.

It frightened Lydia to think it, but the thought refused to fade. She gave in. *Okay, so I'm helpless by myself, too. Glad I'm not alone.*

Then Alan and the Delta employee lifted her out of the safe quiet car and placed her into a one-size-fits-all wheelchair that felt hard as a church pew when the preacher went past noon. Alan kept jabbering. "So sudden, and we don't do sudden very well. Jesus, not at all, you see." The cars were double-loud in the corridor, the exhaust concentrated like nerve gas, things about the world Lydia had forgotten while at home with her soft lights, open windows, and flowing curtains. Everything out here was about moving yourself, keeping up. Dependence on someone else was a luxury and an obstacle.

The Delta employee tried to keep from looking at Lydia, paid attention to the chair or Alan instead. No one did that when she wore the prosthetics. Being herself made her feel not like herself at all. So goddamn weak.

And then the employee pushed her inside as Alan shouted that he would be right back after parking the car. Lydia felt like she would fall out of the chair. Too many people taking side glances with their heads on the move. Even though they couldn't help it, she hated them, every last fucking one.

"Anywhere you'd like to wait?" the employee asked. She leaned close to Lydia's ear.

"By that bench is fine."

"Which bench?"

"The one I'm looking at."

"I'm sorry, please. I'll take you over and you can lead me." The woman started forward without waiting for an answer. If Alan were there, he would know automatically. Strange how she realized it after all that time, now that he wasn't there. She wanted to tell him nice things, stop the criticism for a while to tell him all the little points she had held back, thinking praise only made a person lazy and deluded. However, the time was right. On the plane, she would shower him with kudos.

The woman got the right bench on the third try. It was the one facing the rest of the terminal and the sliding glass doors they had come through. She didn't want anyone to sneak up from behind while she was distracted by the types of luggage people carried in line.

"This fine?" the Delta woman said.

"It'll do. Don't any of these wheelchairs have straps to hold me up?"

"I can check into that," she was already trying to step away.

Lydia knew she wouldn't check. "Please. Much appreciated." *I bet you're a she-male, bitch.* The thought gave her a tiny fake smile of her own. She set her eyes on the sliding doors, hoping Alan would come back quickly, hoping Megan, Terry and Lancaster didn't find her first. Finally feeling…

…simply…

…alone.

And the crowd was far away, like the fuzzy background filled with extras in a movie. The noise didn't have a thing to do with her, bells and whistles and robotic female voices on the intercom.

She looked left, people pulling their wheeled luggage while talking on cell phones. Looked right, a line at the security gate waiting to get into the concourse. That was the only moves she had short of looking up, down, closing her eyes, or shouting at the top of her lungs.

So instead she focused on the sliding doors ahead of her and *willed* Alan to come back to her. *Lovers do it all the time, something psychic about how we connect. Come back, please, to be my arms and legs and heart.*

The Delta employee made eye contact. Lydia blinked. That woman was talking to someone. A tall man, grayish hair and a thick mustache. Security guard uniform. He lifted a walkie-talkie, spoke a few words, then listened for an answer. The Delta woman shook her head. The guard then turned to Lydia, then back to the woman.

Lydia remembered the cops at her house. As soon as word got out, of course, Jesus, she was easy to find. Alan wasn't invisible, either, but fat is a little more anonymous than "no arms or legs."

Hurry, Alan, we're out of time.

Another security guard showed up beside the first one. Young and thick-muscled, deep brown skin and bald. No way to deny it anymore, because the glances were obvious—it wasn't like she could *run* or anything. They knew who she was.

When the New Orleans police cruiser pulled up to the curb outside, Lydia thought, *We're not going to Miami, sweetie.*

Alan watched from above, the second-floor entrance from the parking garage, as the police surrounded Lydia and led her away. After finding a parking spot on the second level, Alan smoothed his hand across the trunk like he was in a commercial, trying to ignore the dented bumper and broken light. Stupid. It was goddamned Monte Carlo. He was on to better cars, a Lexus or a Benz. Still, it was a beautiful machine and he wouldn't be coming back to it.

With all the traffic and noise in and out all day, the smell of the guy in the trunk could be covered up for a while, he hoped. Eventually, someone would notice the car or the smell. By then, Alan would call himself *Trent* or *Richard* and grow his hair longer, even wear a beard. Fuck diets, he'd get his fat sucked out, get one of those Bowflex machines and build the muscles.

He tossed the keys in a trashcan, thinking someone would be along to carry the bag away long before the car appeared suspicious. Let them pry open the trunk. No reason to make it easier. Then he found a pay phone and called the police, said, "I think that legless woman on the news is at the airport right now."

It was a wild guess the story had already made the news. He decided to make the call when he saw the eyes of the security guard at the door as they lifted Lydia from the car to the wheelchair. Curiosity was one thing, but Alan knew suspicion when he saw it. Rather than risk both of them getting caught, he thought maybe they wouldn't go as hard on Lydia alone. She was brainwashed, that's the story she would use, and in her condition the cops would certainly cut her a break—not like she could help it if a guy Alan's size wanted to take her anywhere.

One thing he hoped was that she wouldn't roll over on him. He loved her enough to let her go back to her comfortable life next to the windows and the curtains at home. Life on the run wasn't that easy. Besides, she'd never guess he was the one who called.

As the chair disappeared from sight down the corridor, he felt a hole inside suddenly, the magnetic force cutting him off. More cops were on the way, probably. And someone was waiting for Alan to return, too.

Back to the car? Cut his losses and drive out of here? Unless the cops were watching those exits.

No, better to keep going forward. Into the terminal and the mass of people where he could hide in plain sight if he was lucky.

Then why are you standing here about to throw up?

Because it was the last time he'd see her. Obsessive, too intense, deadly, but in the end, he really loved her.

Alan stepped over to the escalator and jogged down.

THIRTY-THREE

Lancaster was taking a piss and Megan was in line to buy yogurt when the cops rolled Lydia past Terry. She was downcast, walled-off, didn't notice Terry at all. Then again, she'd never gotten a good look at him before. He thought about running into the bathroom and grabbing Lancaster, or maybe shouting at Megan, but after a few moments of staring after the cops and the wheelchair, Terry took another glance at Megan, then the men's room door, before he took off after Lydia. Telling those two about her would cause some kind of riot, and the woman didn't deserve it. If he kept up with Lydia, Crabtree would show soon enough.

Terry stepped into the wake of the chair, carefully at first, afraid his partners would notice him sneaking off and break his legs. No worries, though. Megan was typically self-absorbed, staring off into space at the pictures in her head.

He followed about twenty feet behind, hiding in the clumps of people dragging wheeled luggage and garment bags, some teen girls with worn backsacks hugging pillows, more people in suits on cell phones than should be allowed. Terry studied the cops, learning what type of credential he needed to get into the room where they were taking Lydia. He could take her some coffee. A Sky Cap could do that. He needed a vest, a large coffee, a straw, and the names of those cops. Yeah, back to the con. He felt confident, young. Jesus, the past few days had sucked so bad, he felt like this uncle of his, a guy who got religion in his forties and went from an old biker to a goddamn prude in about a week. Shaved his beard, tossed the old AC/DC albums out (didn't even offer them to Terry), and became a guy who preached pretty much non-stop. His wife, who had wanted the guy to settle down some in the first place, upped and left him after a year of his new Southern Baptist "Head of my Household" routine. And Terry finally understood a little, being scared of something so much—be it hell, death, or your best friend—it could change a man into a straight arrow.

Terry glanced over his shoulder. The crowd was thick enough he couldn't tell if Lancaster and Megan were after him or not. Fuck it. If they caught him, he'd make up something, try to get Lancaster preoccupied, tell him, *I thought I saw Crabtree eating a taco.*

The corridor angled left. The cops took Lydia through a side door, unmarked, equipped with a card-reader lock. All right, not a problem. Terry decided someone else would use the door soon enough. Look the guy over, his uniform, all that, then get a card off someone dressed like him. Usually, he needed Lancaster to help with parts like this, taking something by force. It wasn't like Terry was a weakling—he was strong enough, and he had the element of surprise. The only thing to worry about was leading his mark to a security blind spot since airports were worse than prisons now regarding surveillance.

There was a bar nearby where he could watch and wait, even hide from Lancaster should he need to. He pulled a wad of bills from his pocket. Lancaster had threatened most of the money away from him before they left Biloxi, never did. Terry still had about thirty bucks. While walking to an open stool near the back, he wondered why he really wanted to talk to Lydia anyway. Terry wasn't after revenge like Lancaster, wasn't looking to fool her like Megan. It was more like he felt they had a lot in common. Lydia must've had a powerful pull to get Crabtree, a coward if he'd ever seen one, to kill for her. She was running a con, and he wanted to talk to her about, maybe learn a few things, always looking to better his game.

How long of a conversation could it be, though? Ten minutes in an airport holding room before the cops came back? Terry fought a grin and shook his head. If he was good enough to talk his way in (and he *was*, no doubt), he was damned sure good enough to talk his and Lydia's way out.

Lancaster walked out of the men's room, the cast torn off his forearm except for a ragged piece still around his bicep where the bullet had shredded muscle and bone. He found Megan wandering in a little circle, small cup of vanilla yogurt clenched in her upturned palm.

"Little M&M's on it?" Lancaster said.

Megan blinked, kept looking around. "Terry's gone."

"Where'd he go?"

"No, that's it. He didn't tell me. I bought this and then he was gone, quick as that."

Lancaster turned his head left, then right, a long time passing. He slid his hands together, still moist between the fingers from washing. The nerves in his hand were on the fritz, pinpricks and electric pops. "He'll come back."

"So we just stand here until he does?"

Megan was getting a little pissy. Because she was scared Terry would turn them in, or because she knew Lancaster would be angry, or because she wanted as much control over Terry as Lancaster seemed to have—whatever. Lancaster didn't want to have a fucking *conversation* about it. Before too much longer, she'd want to know what he was doing going from one room to another. *Why did you go in there? What did you get?* He hadn't been in a real relationship in years, not with a clingy woman who thought she was his equal and all. This one might be heaven-sent, but this was the dirty Earth and she needed to learn how things worked.

Lancaster shrugged and said, "We need the Delta terminal. Come on."

"What about Terry?"

"Delta terminal." He walked off, figured this girl wasn't ready to take a stand. Actually, Lancaster was a little lost without Terry, had a twisty feeling in his gut he didn't want to name. Fear, no, not that. An image in his head of a pitcher getting ready to toss in a slider without a catcher behind the plate. Goddamn it, nobody signaling what to throw, no choices. That left one play—hit the batter. The high heat upside the head.

Megan trotted up beside him, slipped her arm into his. She was different from Terry, not calling the plays, rather waiting for Lancaster to act before saying, *What was that about?*

"Your arm better?" she said.

"Probably as good as it'll ever get."

"Don't say that."

"I'll be like Bob Dole, except I'll hold a gun instead of a pencil."

"But if you can't squeeze the trigger—"

"Intimidate first, surprise later. My other hand, remember."

They walked along the corridor slowly, oblivious to everyone else, who would come within inches before realizing these two weren't moving, get out of their way. Like Sid and Nancy, Kurt and Courtney, Lancaster hearing the music in his head.

Megan was soft and her skin was cool. He liked feeling it against him in this heat, the soupy thick New Orleans air, no better inside than out. He wondered how the rest of her would feel later—if there *was* a later—when he would fuck her. He hoped she was hairy down there. The hairy girls were more animal, liked it rough. He wondered if she would howl or grunt. She'd better scratch, too, because sex wasn't good without blood or bruises. Lancaster pulled her tighter, glanced down as she smiled wide. Those eyes were hard. Good.

Up ahead, the corridor opened into a large round hub, a Cajun cooking supplies store across from the Delta ticket counters, the middle filled in with blue vinyl benches and the arrivals/departures boards. Past that, a line formed at the metal detectors leading to the gates. Lancaster got a feel for the security, and he guided Megan towards the board, lazy and disinterested. The Miami flight was delayed, now leaving thirty minutes past schedule.

Megan said, "You know what? We ought to take the tickets when we find Crabtree. We can go to Miami."

Lancaster shook his head. "You need I.D. for that. And I don't want to fly."

"Why not?"

"It's a big shake-up. You're here, suddenly two hours you're a thousand miles away. It messes up your inside map, see? Driving, I can follow along and get a grip. You can adjust gradually."

"I don't get it."

"Being in New Orleans feels different from, say, Houston. If you drive, you can process it all. You fly, it's too quick a jump. I'm still on New Orleans time."

They staggered a little walking to a bench, trying to walk all tangled up. A nasty bubble-assed woman in tight jeans sat on the other end, a toddler in her lap, an older kid buzzing around. The woman ignored all that.

Megan said, "That where you want to go? Houston?"

"Shit, I hate Houston. I don't know where to go. We'll ask Terry later."

"If he doesn't come back?"

Lancaster stared at the fat woman beside them and said, "Then we'll follow him. Right before I kill him, I'll ask him where I should go."

THIRTY-FOUR

"It doesn't compute, him dropping you here and then taking off. You don't have a ticket or anything." The detective sat next to Lydia on her side of the desk and talked low, reasonably.

Two others stood in the room, somebody's office, it looked like. Papers in mid-read on the desk when they commandeered it for the interrogation. A uniformed guard manning a camcorder, a Fed, both quiet. Probably there to see the freak, Lydia thought. She had been here for an hour before the detective came in, Lydia not said a word unless they asked, *You okay?* and, *Is this all right?* when they moved her chair. She whispered, *Fine, thanks*, and went right on staring at her lap.

"Lydia," the detective said. Using her first name like that, *Lydia*, like that would soften her. "I know it's been tough for you, being held against your will, having to witness what happened in your home. I wish I could do something about it."

So, the angle was to trick her into thinking they considered her the victim when all along they knew she was an accomplice. Or maybe they really didn't know. Jesus, if that were true...

"Detective Broussard will recover quickly. However, Officer Lanier didn't make it. He passed on."

Lydia turned to him now, couldn't read him. A good detective, played this game many times before. Lydia was a quick study and hid her panic. They had her and Alan pegged as cop killers.

"We need to find him before he hurts anyone else." The detective took a peek at his papers, mostly blank, Lydia saw. "Crabtree. Alan. We've seen him pop up before, but something desperate must have happened for him to go this far. He's usually as far away from the dangerous stuff as you can get."

Lydia wondered if Alan was in the next room or one similar to this one. He probably walked right into the trap, not realizing she'd been made. How long would it take Alan to roll on her, save himself? Jesus, and he just might.

If she kept her mouth shut, they had no fuel at all. She knew the best attorneys, some of them friends. Keep it together. No expressions, no words.

"You know about Randy Tompkins, right?"

Lydia shook her head. Couldn't help it, so she kept on, "No, that's not anyone I know."

"We think Crabtree killed him. He was with Tompkins' partner in Hattiesburg in a car rented in your name. It hit a fire truck. After towing it, we checked out the trunk, found Tompkins dead inside. He'd been shot. Remember? That's why the police came to your house."

Lydia thought she should shrug or something. It worked better with arms. Without, it threw her off-balance, so she sat still and quiet.

The Fed's cell phone chirped. He answered it, listened, then tried to lean and take notes with his free hand. The paper shifted, the notes more like wild scrawl.

He got to "All right," and closed his phone. Then he spoke to the detective. "Tickets purchased earlier this evening through Delta, a flight to Miami, charged to the Discover card of Ronnie Whipps, Lydia's late husband."

The detective sat straighter, hands on his thighs. "Well, he even charged one of your cards, Lydia. I can't imagine what it was like, this lunatic busting up your life. I'm so sorry. Did he hurt you? Would you like us to get some paramedics in here?"

Lydia shook her head. "I'm fine, really."

"We can get you to a hospital."

"No, please, thank you."

"Why Miami?"

She almost answered, caught herself on the B in *Because*, then swallowed hard and lapsed back into silence.

The detective, a guy in ruffled clothes with a dark mustache and no-rim glasses, sighed like he was in a local play. He stood and walked to the door, stuck his head out and told someone, "Bring those in."

Then he hung there, half-out and half-in, waiting while the camcorder light kept glowing and the cop running it watched Lydia in the viewscreen rather than ogle her in person.

Don't be afraid to look, Lydia wanted to say. *I don't mind.*

The detective pulled back inside, bringing the door open with him.

Another man in a classier suit entered followed by another uniformed cop, a woman. They each carried a large plastic bag. Whatever was inside the bags pressed out hard, and the woman had to turn hers a couple times before she got it through the doorway. They set the bags on the table and stepped to the other side of the office.

The detective's eyebrows were high like Spock's before he reached into one of the bag pulled out a leg. A rubber leg. Lydia's.

It was clean, in good condition. She could almost feel it, all goosebumpy from the cold air in the office. It should really be under her skirt, in a nice blue thigh-high stocking.

The detective kept speaking as he brought out the other leg, then both arms. "As soon as we got the call it was you, I had these cleaned up and sent over. We had already gotten all the use out of them as evidence, prints and fibers. If you want, maybe the officer could help you reattach them before we continue?" He pointed to the woman who had brought one of the bags in, the young cop with her honey-brown hair braided past her shoulders. She tried to ignore Lydia, looked as if she thought amputation was contagious.

Lydia wanted those legs, those arms, wanted to feel less of a freak. Wheelchair bound, okay, like when Megan first thought Lydia was a quad. While people could empathize, even imagine themselves as quads or paraplegics, they could certainly never think of losing all their limbs at once.

Tell them it was all Alan, a brutal man. A murderer. Tell them I was helpless, him bringing death into the tranquil home I worked so hard on to bring me some sort of peace.

It was not a trap, she tried telling herself. Instead, the exit. All they needed was information, and it would be over, and she could go back home, maybe without Alan there to help. Somewhere along the way, eventually, there would be another.

Yes. I'll tell them.

A knock on the door. A man opened the door, stuck his head in. The cop pulled it open full. The new man wore a blue shirt, black slacks, and a vest with SECURITY on the front. This was a blond guy, about thirty, several days of stubble, a bruise coloring one side of his face. He glanced at the others in the room, a little uncertain of himself.

"You need something?" the detective asked.

The security man nodded. "They told me, since I've had some experience."

"What the hell are you talking about?"

The security guy leaned close to the detective's ear. While whispering, he brought a plastic container from behind his back, showed the detective, who said, "Ah, yeah. I got you."

The detective asked everyone to leave the room, lingering a moment to ask, "Shouldn't we let a woman do this?"

"Experience. I had a sister, you know. Soccer injury."

The detective nodded and left the room, closing the door behind him. The security man twisted the blinds closed, checked the camcorder, still looked nervous.

"What was that about?" Lydia said.

"I told them I was here to help you use the bathroom." He waved the bottle a little. Then he leaned in very close and said, "Do you think the room is bugged?"

Lydia shook her head, said, "I can't say."

"Well, please, tell me you have to go do number two anyway. Can't take a shit in here, can you?"

He held her on a toilet in the ladies room that had been cleared specifically for them. Lydia didn't need to shit, but kept up the illusion. As this new security guy had rolled her to the restroom, guard walking ahead, he whispered, "You want to get out of here?"

"What do you mean?"

"Leave. Get away from the cops."

Lydia wanted her arms and legs. A bathroom break, and then they could have the story out of her, and then she'd get her limbs. Something wasn't quite normal about this guy, not a typical security guard.

"You think you can get me out of here? Know all the tricks on minimum wage? No, they pay more now. Federal."

Then they were facing each other, her on the toilet, the man's hands softer than Alan's. He said, "Don't freak out when I tell you this, all right? I forgot that you haven't seen me much. You know the guys who sold Crabtree his car?"

Lydia gave him straight-eyes and her full attention.

"Do you?"

She nodded. "Terry and Lancaster."

"Well," he said. "I'm Terry. Please, don't scream. I'm okay."

"You're security?"

"You're shitting me, right? I got this off a fag guard. Surprised how easy it is, find one off duty, offer a blow job, and next thing I know, he's taking me to this spot where the cameras can't see."

"You blew him off?"

"No, I got his pants down and knocked him out with a chair. God knows when he'll wake up."

Lydia said, "What do you want?"

He sighed, drooped his head. "I don't know, really. Look, I saw them rolling you down here, and I thought you were so sad. See my face, right?" He pointed to his bruise.

"Yeah, I see."

"This is Lancaster. The guy, I've known him a few years, like together a lot, and he was always a little edgy. Barely this side of psycho, probably. That was okay for what we did. He was muscle, and I ran the games. It was a good living, we got by, no responsibilities."

"Why'd he hit you?"

"I think he's lost it. After he got shot, there's no filter anymore between thinking it and doing it. Jesus, he's killing people. Gonna kill your boyfriend, you know."

Lydia said, "Unless the cops catch him first. Yeah, that's all over now."

"Lancaster's hooked up with that girl you picked up. So, fuck, I've got to get out of here."

"And you want me along?"

Terry grinned. "Sure, if you want to go. We'll figure something out."

She breathed through her mouth and wished it were a dream. Terry wasn't bad looking, a little paunchy.

Arms, legs, home.

And then what? Cops watching her every move?

The curtains, and the perfect limbs. That's the real me.

No, the real Lydia, she thought, liked to have control. If Alan wasn't taking her to Miami, then this frat boy could at least take her somewhere else. He was trainable.

She smiled. "Can you get rid of the guard?"

He smiled back. "I've come this far."

THIRTY-FIVE

Alan banked on dumb, tired airport personnel. He wanted on that plane to Miami, knew in his heart that Lydia wouldn't rat him out. So he locked himself in a bathroom stall and rifled through his pockets until he found a pen and a nail clipper, one with a little file on it. He wanted to change Ronnie's name on the ID and boarding pass to Randall, thinking maybe the security brigade would be zoned in on finding Ronnie and let this blip pass by. Fuck the little voice in his head telling him it was hopeless and he should be in the car already, putting much space and even more space between himself and this airport.

Hey, it's Miami.

Still, why not drive it in? Hadn't he told Lydia something similar at the hotel? Maybe eighteen hours on the road, less chance of getting noticed than trying to muscle into a plane.

I want to be there quicker.

Like a kid, this side of him taking over and trying to make this ID real-looking, not the work of a nervous guy lifting the laminate and scribbling in a fake name. Changing the Chemistry grade in high school and hoping Dad wouldn't notice. Trying to phony the winning horse's name on another losing ticket.

It never worked.

Here he was, trying again. *If you fall off the horse—ha ha, 'horse'—get right back in the saddle.* Horses, Miami. They mixed nicely. First night in town, he would be at the track, getting the feel of things before laying a few bets. Maybe he could work his way in, somehow. Betting was only an excuse to be near the business anyway. If he couldn't ride them, why not train them? One day, maybe own a thoroughbred.

Alan shook the daydream off and noticed the pen had slipped. He licked his thumb and tried to wipe the line away. It smeared wide. He tried more licking, rubbing, tried toilet paper. Still left with a black stain.

No one will notice, he thought. The card trembled in his fingers and he felt his chest go tight, trying to keep from crying. Everything turning to shit so fast. He squeezed his eyes shut and then blinked tears away. He steadied his hands and tried to copy the computer font on the card with his felt tip. Funny how even though he was trying hard to make this work, staying at the airport felt a lot like giving up.

Alan waited until the line was a little thick, still moving quickly. Part of him was hoping the guards would go ahead and cuff him, slow his heart down a bit. The guy looking at his boarding pass and ID must've been a retired guy, ancient and skeletal, a face like Charlton Heston, in a blue sweater that swallowed him. A quick glance down, back up, and he handed the stuff back to Alan.

"Thank you," was all he got.

"Sure," Alan said. He moved ahead, two black women, the younger heavy on make-up, behind the bag screener, deep in conversation, while a white woman with acne asked him to step through the metal detector. He did. Nothing went off. Alan had left his belt and a handful of change in the bathroom stall. They ran the wand around him, asked him to lift his shoes. Still okay. He was free to keep going, find the gate, and wait for boarding. Only twenty minutes left. If he could keep the momentum going before the alert was sent out, maybe, *maybe*, he'd be on the flight to Miami and free. No longer a killer, the first thing he decided. And he would call himself Ronnie until he could find some new ID, maybe call himself Paul. Paul was a peaceful name. Nobody bothered guys named Paul. Paul Newman, *Cool Hand Luke*, that said it all. Play cool. Alan had never seen that movie, thought about renting it.

Megan caught a glimpse of Crabtree fading into the line at the concourse security check. She pointed and said, "There!"

Lancaster hopped off the bench, slapping Megan's arm out of the way. He took a few quick steps that direction but then stopped. Megan eased beside him.

"What?" she said.

"He gets through security, we can't touch him. They don't let people in there unless you fly."

They posed all pissed for a moment, the way the cool kids were supposed to, the slumped fidgety shit. Waves of people crashed through and Lancaster took inventory, all the doors and guards—those guards now paying attention to him.

"Wanna rush the security?" he said.

Megan sighed. "Baby, we said—"

"Only if possible, right? Now it doesn't look possible."

"Why do you have to do this anyway? Leave him alone. He's a sad, sad man."

"I already told you why."

"You did not."

Lancaster turned on her, angry eyes. Then he softened. "You're right. Must've been Terry. I told Terry."

Where the hell is he? Lancaster thought. Earlier, he was supposing the guy took a walk, bought a beer or went after somebody's wallet. A while later, no word from him, Lancaster realized the little prick abandoned ship, the easy way out. He didn't like the way it felt, like he was mad enough to rage on the closest person and then desperate like he'd forgotten everything he knew. Planning stuff was Terry's job. Shit. Now what?

More than planning, though, it was his *friend*, man. Friends fight, but come on, like he really hurt Terry enough to send him running. Pussy boy needed to toughen up, that was all. So he ran off, left Lancaster in the lurch. What kind of friend was that? Dragged him out of the hospital when logic said *Get lost*. It comes to the real deal, finally in arm's length of Crabtree, and *that's* when he bolts?

"We need Terry," Lancaster said.

"Jesus, he's probably fifty miles gone by now. You don't *need* him, because I'm here now."

He laughed at her. Those guards took double notice. He laughed loud.

"Bitch, you got a plan?" he said. "You better than Terry now, so don't be jerking my chain. Tell me the plan. How do we get to Crabtree?"

"I told you—"

Right in her face, spitting words, "What you told me was bullshit. What you said was all about getting your pretty ass out of here. What I'm *telling* you now is that I want a goddamn good plan to go cap Crabtree because no one—*no fucking one*—does what he did to me and gets away with it."

Megan teared up, eyes glossy. "You're insane."

"You think?"

"Crazy."

He grinned and shook his head slowly, her eyes following left and right. "You had this image all cooked up in your head, didn't you? Had me pegged like Travolta in *Fever*, right? Fucking women, you're only good enough for dick sucking because you're too stupid for anything else. Shit, wanting some fairy tale? This ain't a movie. This ain't no party, this ain't no disco, this ain't no foolin' around."

Megan balled her fists. "You want a plan? How's this? Fuck security. I'll bet you can get out on the tarmac, grab an orange vest, then wait for him at the plane."

Lancaster kept the stare intense. He was somewhere else, thinking about that idea. Finally said, "That's pretty good. Shit. That's not half bad."

THIRTY-SIX

Can a walk look guilty? Alan worked on making his walk very innocent as he passed several more security guards on the way to his gate. He also passed a kiosk selling pretzels, and he was starving. They sold popcorn, too, smelled good. He groped in his pocket, a wad of bills in there. He stopped and turned around, walked back to the kiosk and bought an expensive box of popcorn and a Diet Coke. It was habit, the diet stuff. The taste never grew on him. Eating handfuls and walking at the same time, Coke bottle tucked between his chest and arm, he dropped kernels and thought maybe the guards would tell him to clean up his mess. No one gave a shit. He found his gate, a pretty packed flight, lot of older people, looked like it was group or something, matching T-shirts that Alan didn't bother to read.

He sat near the window and looked out at the tarmac, big jets lined up across the way. No plane at the Miami gate yet. Jesus, it was time to board, where was the fucking plane? He craned his neck to get a look at the monitor behind the desk—*Now 10:05.* Alan checked his watch. 9:20. Another forty minutes until boarding, and too much could go wrong. He lifted another handful of popcorn to his mouth, not caring how much he dropped, pieces falling on his lap, the chair next to him. Swigged the Diet Coke, wishing it were beer.

Lydia won't tell them a thing.

She wouldn't have to, though. She wasn't a Jane Doe. A couple of calls, trace some credit cards, bam zoom, call it all off.

Where's the goddamned plane?

A phone behind the desk rang. The attendant picked it up. She was tall, like Lydia had been before the accident, all the photos she showed him. The woman at the desk had long brown hair to her waist, a narrow serious face. Alan couldn't make out the conversation but she was sure intense, and then she looked at the passengers waiting, found Alan. She blinked and turned away, speaking into the phone quickly.

Alan checked his watch. Only two minutes had passed. Hands all slick again. He wondered if the people nearby could smell the sweat on him. Something like dead flowers, sickly sweet. He focussed on a jet nearly. A big sucker, maybe a 757. Too many people on cell phones, couldn't hear himself think.

A voice over the speakers, "Passenger Whipps, please report to gate D-7 immediately. Passenger Whipps for Delta flight 405 to Miami, report to gate D-7. It's urgent."

Alan barely moved his head, enough to see the attendant set the handset down, the speakers clicking off. A security guard standing with her now. Jesus, that was fast. The attendant's back was to Alan, the guard scanning the seats over her shoulder until he found Alan, obvious she was pointing him out. *The fat guy, the sweaty one with the popcorn by the window.*

If he ignored the call, how could they know for sure he was pretending to be who he claimed to be? Stupid, since they probably had photos and his sheet and fingerprints and god knew what else. Until they actually approached and dragged him away, there was no reason to give up yet.

"Excuse me, sir?"

Another goddamn guard. Where did they come from? Beamed in from space or shot up from tunnels?

"Sir?"

On his left. Alan turned to face him, a scrawny guy with a skimpy mustache. He probably thought the women liked it. "Yeah?"

"You're Mr. Whipps?"

Shit. "Yes, officer. Is there a problem?"

"We need to talk to you. Your wife, you know she's here?"

Alan wrenched his neck around, leaned forward in his chair. "She all right?"

The officer, hands on his belt, said, "Come with me, please."

"I beg your pardon?"

The officer rolled his eyes, reached for Alan's arm. Once the guy touched him, Alan thought, it was over. Time to play another card. Alan stood, took a step back, finger wagging the guard. "I don't like this little guessing game. You say there's a problem, I want to know what it is."

He quick-stepped around carry-on luggage littering the floor, made it to the desk, right in the attendant's face. If she was freaked, she hid it. The other guard, beefy compared to the mustache-boy, didn't move. If they weren't grabbing him, throwing him against a wall and spraying shit in his face, Alan thought maybe he still had a chance.

"Excuse me," he said. "This young man here isn't really being very helpful, and I'd like some information. This is an important flight for me, and I don't like games. What's going on?"

The attendant spoke like a recorded phone operator, everything the same level of ease. "You'll have to speak to security about that. I don't have any details."

"Can you get them? If we're boarding in a half-hour, I don't want to go all the way out and then have to rush to get back, re-do security, all that."

The big guard finally spoke. "Sir, don't concern yourself with that right now. Just come with us."

The mustache-boy stood behind him. Passengers watched them because they were more interesting than CNN. Still, no one had demanded anything. It was all very calm. All the news he'd heard, Alan figured they wouldn't put up with any unruly passengers, argumentative passengers, or even those who sighed too loud. Jesus, what was the play now?

Alan said, "I have a heart condition. This isn't helping. So what I'm going to do is sit over there behind that thing." He pointed to a bench of three seats by the desk, partially hidden from view by a blue divider. "When you people feel like playing straight with me, you can do it here."

He brushed past the big guard and walked to the bench, sat down, took up most of two cushions. Left his popcorn in the waiting area. An exaggerated glance at his watch again, big head shake. The guards stayed where they were, the little one lifting a walkie-talkie and mumbling into it.

Unless they forced him out of there, Alan guessed he had five more minutes to think of a plan. Miami was fading fast. Lancaster was probably watching from the fringes, ready to pop him soon as the chance showed itself. A body in the trunk of his Monte Carlo. He was out of luck fighting with the guards if he tried to run for it, wouldn't get through the security gate.

Think!

And then the door to the gate opened. The plane had arrived, already letting off passengers. The first group came through the door, luggage on wheels in tow, jackets draped over arms and shoulders, every one of them looking frazzled.

Maybe inside the airport he was out of luck, but outside? Alan turned to the guards, both with cold eyes intent on him. He waved over one. The mustache-boy stepped to his side, leaned over.

Alan pulled a Pepcid from his pocket, showed the guard. "I have to take this, keeps the blood pressure down. Would you mind getting me a glass of water? I feel dizzy."

"Sure. Be right back." The guard headed for a kiosk.

Easier to run from one than two.

And here we go...

THIRTY-SEVEN

Security like a motherfuck, Lancaster thought. He was losing hope fast, trying to find a way onto the tarmac without being noticed. Megan trailed behind, barely saying a word since she gave him the new plan, and sure as shit didn't bother touching him. That was fine. She'd touch him later whether she wanted to or not.

Then he laughed, a bark, already thinking about later when he needed to concentrate on the moment. It wasn't like he was going to survive anyway. Dumb bitch putting ideas in his head. Once he fucked Crabtree up good, the security would descend on him like locusts. God, man, he wanted a gun. If he was extinguished, he wanted to take a few pigs with him. Not a chance. Things were tight in the shiny new police state. He though, *Can't a man even bring a gun to an airport? Old West folks had it made.*

Up and down the halls for a while, Megan in tow with her arms crossed and feet stamping. Finally, down the escalator. The baggage claim was mostly empty, so he stopped there, looked far and wide.

"What?" Megan said. The pout on this girl, Jesus.

"How about climb through there." He pointed a finger-gun at a baggage carousel.

"No way. We can't do that."

"Why? Because it's illegal?"

Megan held back, calmed down, said, "That doesn't lead out, though. It goes into a maze or something."

"Then it leads out. All the trucks that take stuff to the planes, we can grab one of those before they catch on."

"Yeah, that's just it. They *will* catch on."

Lancaster popped his lips, swooned his fingers like magician. "Like I've said all along. You can take off now, you want. No biggie."

Megan was close to tears, and Lancaster wanted to backhand her.

Love at first sight always ended up like this—never the beach and the sunset, *always* the twisted crash and burn. He closed his eyes and wished she'd vanish like a ghost. If Terry were here, he would probably have a good escape route. Should've listened to the guy instead of gone all *Blaze of Glory* on him.

She said, "I thought you were my new life, not the end of it."

"End of the new life? End of the old?"

"End period."

He *pfft* a sharp breath, said, "They won't shoot you. Look at you. They'll want you for strip-searching, turn the hose on you. And that's before the guards in prison fuck you bloody most nights. Far from dead, least until your looks fade."

She was slack-jaw stunned. "I can't believe you just said—"

"Two choices," he said, holding up a *V* and showing her the front and back of it. "You come with, or you go bye-bye. And you have to decide, mmmmmmmmm, now."

And Lancaster snapped his fingers.

And he turned away like he was James fuckin' Dean all the sudden.

Megan watched him take a few jive steps before she felt the pull—magnetic, urgent—and shuffled behind him.

Right up to the empty baggage carousel, the worn black conveyer belt, the scuffed plastic flap, without pausing to reconsider, Lancaster stepped up, crouched down, and crawled through. Megan followed, a bit delicately.

Lancaster anticipated what happened next, the second he was through the flap.

The airport went apeshit.

Alarms donging pleasantly followed by a voice asking people to evacuate the terminal.

Lancaster hoped he still had enough surprise on his side. First guy he saw with a gun, he was zooming in. Disarm, deactivate, no time to dismember. He visualized it, microseconds seeming like hours, until he was game-day ready to emerge into the bowels of the airport.

The one guard gone for water, Alan sat still until a wave of passengers from the exiting plane made a nice shield for him. He was up, weaving, fast as he'd ever been, already inside the door when the beefy guard shouted *Hey, you!*

The door was swinging closed, and Alan hustled for the handle, but it kicked open again, banged his shoulder, and he nearly collided with an annoyed guy in a business suit. He brushed past, faced a steady stream of people, the corridor was wide enough that he didn't have to squeeze through tight holes.

Halfway down, he heard the guard's voice behind him, "*Stop that man!*" Alan hoped it would scare people rather than rev them up, though the way things had changed, everyone in coach might tackle him, helping defend America, getting a spot on *Today* to tell Katie Couric how heroic they felt.

Instead, these people looked confused. One woman let out *Oh my God*. The others went limp. One look at Alan was enough—*Shit, guy's bigger than me. Shoot his ass.* He kept moving, creeping, rolling past like was tripping, hoping the pilot wasn't some armed maverick waiting to take him out. Ahead to the right was a pile of valet bags, an attendant sorting through as a handful of passengers crowded around. They blocked the door leading to stairs leading to the tarmac. Alan decided to fuck *Excuse me* and bowl them over if necessary.

They watched him rush ahead, only realizing at the last minute that this wasn't a good place to be. The passengers ducked inside the plane or flattened against the wall. Alan tripped over a folded stroller, nearly tumbled, grabbed the attendant and steadied himself.

The guard was coming fast from the other end of the corridor, Alan turning to see the guy only twenty feet away. Nineteen. Eighteen.

Alan wrapped his arm around the attendant's neck, some wrestling hold, which stopped the guard at fifteen feet, wild guess. Too damn close, anyway. That's when the alarms went off, faint in this corridor away from the terminal, but still heartstopping, Alan doing fear and extra sweat, not listening to macho guard yelling at him, gun straight. No time for a stand-off. Alan pushed the attendant towards the guard and reached behind him, pushed the door open, and nearly fell outside.

The engine whine was louder than anything he'd ever heard, white noise wiping out the alarms, the corridor shouting, the workers on the ground scrambling. Vests and baggage trains and orange sticks and ear protection, Lights flashing in the fading light, world going to gray, and Alan took the stairs in three big steps, came down hard on an ankle, felt it like a snap. He only let the pain reach him for a second before he ducked low and took off under the wing across the tarmac. Other planes stopped now where they were when the alarms rang—a line heading out to the runway, another incoming, almost to its gate.

The ankle, every step like a blade stabbing it. Alan kept going. He was disoriented. He wanted to find the Veterans Boulevard side, make a run for it where he could hitch a ride or blend into the crowds and traffic. To get that far, he needed to find the runway, find the parking garage. The goddamn Delta terminal wasn't giving directions, hiding the world beyond its walls.

Get out there, get a better view.

The ankle hurt like holy shit and he was sure others behind him would be quicker.

Don't think that way. Until they stop you, don't stop.

Voices in your head, Alan thought, were all talk, no action. He kept going, skipping to keep weight off the ankle, speeding him up. A glance behind him. The lights of an airline cart, catching up. They hadn't shot him yet, probably planned to whip around, cut him off. Still until they did, maybe a minute or less, he didn't give up the skipping, skipping, skipping to freedom. The guards in the cart would get him to the ground, clamp the cuffs on, and this would be over. Maybe in prison, he could work in the library, something peaceful. At least he had new bulk, more muscle. No one was going to punk him out. Besides, regardless of three murders, if they could even pin all three on him, he could still turn on Lydia. She was the mastermind, the bigger fish. And all his dirt on the businessmen and politicians he used to work for, little clean up and blackmail jobs, had to be worth something to reduce his time.

Thinking like that, he slowed his pace, the skip going to a slo-mo gallop before he stood still and raised his hands, tried to make it easy on everyone.

Goddamn it if the cart didn't stop, bashed right into him, full speed.

THIRTY-EIGHT

Terry's arm was shoulder deep in a trashcan when the alarms sounded. He and Lydia were in the parking garage at the Monte Carlo, Terry hoping aloud that Crabtree would've ditched the keys in the trash like any low class crook. If it were up to Terry, this guy always talking, the keys would end up farther away, a trash can in a men's room in one of the concourses.

"Hurry," Lydia said, the voice over the speakers and the alarm asking visitors to evacuate the terminal. She wondered what it was all about—her disappearing with Terry or Alan getting iced by Lancaster. Just as quickly, she didn't want to know. This was about survival. Alan, sure, there was love, and that would haunt her. The best she could say was at the end she didn't give him up. Leaving was better than betraying, enough so she would be able to sleep at night.

Terry hit something mushy and recoiled like a scared squirrel. "Gross."

"Look, what about your car?"

Terry lifting the bag from the can, took it over to the wall next to a Seville, a nice hiding spot, and dumped the trash on the ground. The keys tinkled enough for Terry to zero in like sonar.

"Got 'em." He lifted them high and smiled like a goofy frat boy. Lydia remembered Alan describing him like that. It was pretty much spot on.

"Can we go now before we're cornered?"

Terry hurried around to the Monte Carlo, unlocked and opened the passenger door. He helped Lydia into the seat, those too-soft hands not as fumbly as Alan's. He clicked her seatbelt, checked it with a good tug, then shut her door and bopped around to the other side. Terry seemed a hundred degrees happier out of the terminal, ready to go anyplace other than here. He plopped into his seat, same silly grin, and cranked up.

"Ready?" He lifted the parking stub from the dash, wiggled his fingers deep in his pocket and came out with a few one-dollar bills. "Have to pay to park, you know."

"Just drive, please. What if they stop us?"

"This might be one time where I won't bother trying to talk our way out. Hopefully, they'll take the money and raise the gate. If not, we bust through the gate."

Lydia smiled despite her tone. The façade breaking down, but she didn't feel bad about it. This cocky little bastard, ready to be molded, no problem. As Terry made his way out of the maze and onto the ramp heading out, she said. "As long as there's more to that plan."

"There's always more. Where we going, anyway?"

"Far away," Lydia said, more breath than voice. Then, "Someplace warm, though."

Terry nodded. "Sure, sounds nice." He guessed that in a couple hours, she would be overwhelmed by his charm and pretty much agree to Antarctica if he suggested it. Not quite what he had in mind. Not much warmer, either. "Nice and toasty."

"There's a body in the trunk," Lydia said.

"Hey, no problem."

The baggage cart's impact was rough but not fatal. Instead, the worst part was Alan's leg getting caught under the front bumper at a bad angle. The bone snapped and his knee twisted. He fell, smashed his nose on the pavement and went dizzy. Blood on his hands. Face throbbing. Jesus.

He heard a petite voice, familiar, "There, you got him. His leg's broken. Can we *leave* now before we get caught?"

Another rough voice, a man, familiar but ragged. "What made you think I was an eye for an eye, limb for limb guy?"

Alan propped on his elbows, turned his head left, almost threw up. He saw Lancaster approaching, uniformed up in the vest and hat. Megan behind him. The pain went secondary and the escape impulse kicked in. He tried to move forward on his elbows, a few inches. More nausea. He held it all down. Wanted to lift his leg. It wasn't cooperating, his thigh rising, the calf rubbery, hanging down. Seeing that, he finally puked. Blood and puke all over his arms.

Lancaster kicked Alan in the face, full force with a heavy-duty boot. It split his skin from cheek to temple. Another kick to the neck. Another dozen to the shoulder. Working his way down. Alan prayed for the guards to hurry up and get there, prison looking better every second.

"Fucking *shoot* me, you lard-ass son of a whore!" Lancaster kicked as he spoke, rumbling louder than jet noise, working his way down Alan's body. "Ungrateful, we got you that *car* and you *shoot* me?"

Alan tried to speak, all coming out as a cough, bile, more blood and puke.

Lancaster stomped the broken leg.

Kill me, Alan thought, but he wailed high-pitched, old Sammy Hagar yell without girls and sex and rock & roll. Only serious goddamn pain, the kind he'd spent his whole life avoiding.

"*You* followed me to the woods," Alan said, sputtering effort in every word. "*You* were going to kill *me*. Tell me you weren't."

A little more pressure on the leg. "I can kill you anytime I want and you have to like it, not fucking shoot me. Know what you're wishing right now? Wishing you were a better aim, you fat boy freak-fucker."

Megan hopped in place like a little girl. Alan liked that. Must've been close to the light, the pain more cold than anything else, his eyes not wanting to stay open. Where the hell were those guards? It felt like an hour since Lancaster showed up.

"Leave him alone, Lancaster. Jesus, look at him."

"He's still moving, ain't he? Not done yet."

"Were you really going to kill him? Was that why he shot you?"

Another kick, probably ruptured a kidney. Alan's face was swelling, and he had chills. Barely able to glimpse of Lancaster and Megan.

Lancaster took a step back, grinning. Fists ready to strike the final blow. He said, "The guy this asshole shot paid us to keep him alive. We failed. I didn't want to kill Crabtree, you know? I've roughed him up before, sure. That's the way of the jungle. Alpha male keeps the little ones in line." He knelt, inches from Alan's face. "Right, buddy? Wasn't that the way it always went? You never shot me before."

"You deserved it," Alan said.

"I deserved *respect*."

"Okay, you do. Fine, I was wrong," Alan said, trying for sincerity. Don't let the fear do the talking. "I've learned my lesson. It won't happen again."

Lancaster spit at him. "It's too late for that. You're over. But thanks for groveling. Good job. Oh, and I killed your little side show girlfriend, too."

Megan said, "You did not."

"*Shut it!*" He turned back to Alan. "She wasn't there when I did it. Yep, I fucked her to death in the ladies room here."

"You're lying. The police had her."

"Not for long. And then there was me and her, right up her ass, hard as fucking horses, and then I covered her mouth with my hand—"

Alan winced, "No, man..."

"Yeah, and she couldn't claw it off, couldn't shake it off, couldn't kick me, kinda like you right now, except your fat ass doesn't turn me on. And I kept pumping."

Megan pulled at Lancaster's shoulder. "Come on, you know that's bullshit. Leave him alone."

Lancaster grabbed her hair and yanked hard, pulled her face to face, then bit her cheek. She convulsed, slapped him, her cry ramping up as he held on to the skin. He let go, and she had a bloody ring running down her face and neck, still shrilling, top of her lungs.

"*You fuck! You bastard! You never, ever—what the fuck, you, you—*"

He growled and fake-lunged at her, and she retreated to the cart. Lancaster turned to Alan again, put his hand on the back of his neck. "I see the guards finally getting out here. Here they come. Before I snap your neck, I wanted you to know it was all for nothing. She's gone, and the money's gone, and now, you too."

Pressure on the back of Alan's head. Lancaster reached with his other hand. Then the cart backed away from Alan, Megan in the driver's seat.

"Hey, what are you doing?" Lancaster stood and started for the cart. Megan pulled away, a big loop, heading back for the terminal, head on with the approaching guards in SUVs. Then she looped again, full speed right towards Lancaster.

He didn't budge. "Want to play chicken? Is that it? Come on, crack whore. Give it to me. I dare you."

She was fast and steady, no wavering, the sirens and lights behind her catching up fast. Showdown, Lancaster's hands at his sides imitating an itchy fingered cowboy. Alan hoped she didn't lose her nerve.

At the last moment, Lancaster sidestepped the cart, grabbed Megan's shirt from the side and tossed her out like a rag doll. The cart kept rolling, the front tires running over Alan's broken leg before coming to a stop on his body, squeezing him, hard to get the air inside.

Lancaster lifted Megan from the ground, held her at arm's length, and punched her in the face—once, twice, full bore like a boxer. She leaned back, her leg muscles straining, not getting her anywhere.

Then a gunshot, barely registering with the noise. Lancaster dropped Megan and spun silly, head turning left and right and his eyes wide. Another gunshot exploded, his stomach going red, dropping to his knees. Red dots appeared on his head and chest as cops dressed for combat swarmed from behind the SUV pulling to a stop near Alan and the cart on top of him.

Megan found her feet, stumbled a little, barely made it to Alan's side before the cops reached her. She stretched on the pavement in front of him, her forehead touching his. He was barely in the world.

"Hold on, Alan. They're here. You'll be okay."

"I, um…don't feel anything."

"That's your mind protecting you from the pain. Feel my energy, we can share it."

He mumbled something. She couldn't tell he was still alive until he blinked.

"You know he didn't kill Lydia. Oh, I'm so sorry, Alan. I didn't know."

"Issokay…" Alan said. "You okay. Best you coulda…"

A man in a rumpled suit and his pistol drawn made his way to Alan, barking orders at Megan to back away, then getting a good look at the man. "Jesus." Shouted behind him, "Get an ambulance, *right now*."

He got down on one knee beside them. "That freak over there did this?"

Megan said, "You have no idea."

"This Lydia Whipps' kidnapper, or boyfriend, or whatever he was?"

"He's still alive!"

The detective shook his head. "I've seen plenty of folks in plenty of situations. This guy, he's not going to make it."

"You know Lydia? Is she okay? Tell Alan she's okay."

The cop said, "I was questioning her, and she seemed fine, no trauma, just a little quiet."

"Where is she? You've got her in a safe place?"

He shrugged. "She got away. Some blonde security guard rolled her right out from under us. Must be pretty smart, because this place is in serious lockdown mode thanks to that little stunt your boy pulled."

Megan stroked Alan's hair. His eyes now open and unblinking, he was still breathing. Shallow breaths, then catching. A long exhale.

Megan whispered, "You were a good man. She loved you."

Alan didn't take another breath.

EPILOGUE

Six months later

Lydia liked the way the men felt when they were on top of her, their hard cocks urgent and powerful inside her. She gave up trying to memorize their faces weeks ago and instead gave in to fantasy. Alan was still in some of those fantasies, much leaner and more confident, and she shouted his name sometimes. Some of the men didn't like that, and they stopped or they tried to hit her. When that happened, Terry stormed in with a baseball bat and knocked the guy off her, told him his time was up. He protected her that way, and was so gentle when he cleaned her up after each man, washed her with her favorite strawberry/kiwi-scented soap, fixed her hair, changed her silk teddy, sometimes white, sometimes red. He never came on to her, never helped himself. Maybe he didn't find her attractive. Lydia hoped that would change one day. She kept pouring on the sweetness, hoping for his surrender.

When the cops netted her in the airport, Lydia imagined a sexless life. Even if she got out of prison, how would she ever be able to meet another man like Alan? Then Terry suggested they let men pay to be with her, a good way to earn enough money quickly to help them escape to someplace warm. It was taking longer than she expected. Every day, Terry told her they were so much closer, to try being patient. She had lost track of days, lying on this bed, only occasionally being carried throughout the small apartment to watch a little TV (never the news or a talk show, nothing current. Maybe a reality show, a dating show. Terry and she both loved those), or relax in the tub, a rare treat, since Terry had to hold her in there.

She complained about the drafts, since Terry had set them up in an old house divided into two apartments, upstairs and down, in northwest Grand Rapids. The winter winds found the cracks and it was tough to keep their upstairs apartment warm. When they arrived there, it was summer, and Terry raved about the beautiful Michigan summers, assuring Lydia they would be on the way to the tropics before the first snow. As time passed, though, he confessed that the cost of living was taking a little more money than he first anticipated—gas, electric, cable, upkeep on the Monte Carlo, especially getting the back-end repaired.

"I can't keep this up forever," she told him. "Isn't there another way?"

"Sure, if you want to get risky," Terry said.

She couldn't see how having unprotected sex with anonymous men up to ten times a day was any less risky, at least for her. In fact, she had no idea if she was full of disease or pregnant or rotting away from the inside.

All she had were the feelings and the fantasies. Sometimes, considering what prison might have been like, this alternative seemed the better deal. At night, alone, without Alan to tuck her in, she felt disgusting. She often wondered where Alan had escaped to, and hoped he would one day come looking for her.

The next man stood in the doorway. Lydia heard Terry's voice as they discussed price. The sun had set and the light outside the window was fading, so Lydia only saw the silhouette of the man, short and balding in a flannel shirt. He lingered by the bedside looking at her.

"What's your name?" she said.

"Shut up, please. Don't say a word." He dropped his pants and played with himself, breathing getting heavier. Then his free hand reached, rubbed the nub where her left leg used to be. It was the worst thing the men could do. Alan always saw what she had seen—the phantom limbs real as everyone else's if they imagined them to be. He knew the curves, the lengths, all the sensitive spots. These men, it was as if they were slicing their hands right through her skin, touching muscles and bones instead of her reaching arms and shapely legs.

She turned her head to the other side, squeezed her eyes shut, and promised this was the last one. It was time to mold Terry the way she had molded Alan. Terry's resistance had been strong so far, but Lydia still knew some tricks.

The last one.

As the man climbed onto the bed and pushed her silk teddy up, she wondered how many times she had thought that lately. Fifty? A hundred? This time, she meant it.

about the author

Anthony Neil Smith walks the line between pulp and literary writing, forcing them to duke it out on the page. Over twenty of his short stories have been published in lit mags and crime writing zines, and from 1999 to 2004, he was the co-editor/co-creator of the online noir journal *Plots with Guns*. He's also an associate editor with the highly-regarded literary magazine *Mississippi Review's* online edition, where he's put together three special issues featuring crime fiction.

He was born and raised on the Mississippi Gulf Coast, is currently living in Minnesota, and wishes he were tucked away in the corner of a New Orleans bar, scribbling like mad with three crayons and a pocket full of quarters for the poker machine.

Psychosomatic is his first novel.

psychosomatic

psychosomatic

anthony neil smith

Set in Sabon

POINTBLANK is an imprint of Wildside Press
www.pointblankpress.com
www.wildsidepress.com

edited by Juha Lindroos

For more information contact Wildside Press

ISBN: 0-8095-5090-3 (PB)
ISBN: 0-8095-5091-1 (HB)